METAWARS

ORCHARD BOOKS
338 Euston Road, London NW1 3BH
Orchard Books Australia
Level 17/207 Kent Street, Sydney, NSW 2000

First published in 2013 by Orchard Books

ISBN 978 1 40831 461 6

MetaWars is a registered trademark of Awesome Media
& Entertainment Ltd.

Text © Awesome Media & Entertainment Ltd 2013
With special thanks to Steve Lyons

The right of Jeff Norton to be identified as the author of this
work has been asserted by him in accordance with the
Copyright, Designs and Patents Act, 1988.

A CIP catalogue record for this book is available
from the British Library.

1 3 5 7 9 8 6 4 2

Printed in Great Britain

Orchard Books is a division of Hachette Children's Books,
an Hachette UK company.

www.hachette.co.uk
www.jeffnorton.com

METAWARS
BATTLE OF THE IMMORTAL

JEFF NORTON

ORCHARD

For Jack and Patrick – who soared to High Flight

'High Flight'

The poem 'High Flight' was written by John Gillespie Magee Jr., an American poet and aviator who joined the Royal Canadian Air Force in World War II to fly in European combat before the United States had entered the war. He died in 1941 in a midair collision over Lincolnshire.

It is the official poem of both the Royal Air Force and the Canadian Royal Air Force.

Jason Delacroix used to recite it to his young son, Jonah.

1

Jonah leaned on the bow as the boat hurtled through Times Square.

Sam revved the outboard electrical engine of the black, Kevlar-clad dinghy, pointing them across the flooded streets of Manhattan towards Hell's Kitchen. Jonah squinted as the late-afternoon sun tried to blind him. His eyes closed for only a moment, he visualised finally getting his dad back. After two months of incarceration, Jonah was going to bust his father out of his prison.

The flashing neon signs of Times Square took no notice of the floodwater below, and Jonah almost laughed at the strangeness of billboards boasting of luxury goods and exotic metacations while the streets below drowned under a metre of water.

But he didn't.

He knew that when the Guardians flooded Manhattan, the water was trapped inside the city by the same defensive dykes the island nation used to keep out the rising sea levels. Not only would the city face irreparable damage, but he was betraying Manhattan's young president, Lori Weisberg, as well.

He was betraying a friend.

'Jason had better be ready!' shouted Sam, knocking whatever guilt Jonah was wrestling with out of his head and focusing him back on the jailbreak, and his father.

Technically, Jonah's dad was dead. But since Jason had copied his avatar before his death, and Jonah had Uploaded it to the Metasphere, Jonah's father had been able to usurp the mind of Manhattan resident, and celebrity games designer, Lucky Luke Wexler, and had been reborn in his real-world body. But Jason was under house arrest for body theft, and for the past two months, while the Guardians extracted the Metasphere servers of the Western Corner from the old subway tunnels beneath the city, Jonah had been allowed limited visitation rights with his father.

'He will be ready!' called Jonah, hoping it was true. 'It's not safe for him here any more.'

The Uploaded, and therefore Jonah's dad, were under threat from the living. People were angry and afraid, scared to go online for fear of being usurped and outraged with the dead who had stolen the bodies of the living. Jason's prison had protected him from the lynch mobs but it was just a matter of time before the Manhattan residents would force the Co-op Board that ran the island republic to make an example of Jason, attempting an extraction which, if done improperly, could kill both the Uploaded usurper and the host body. So while the Guardians removed the servers of the Western Corner from their secret location, Jonah, Sam and her father, Axel, hatched a daring plot to break Jason out of his building, and all of them out of Manhattan, for good.

Sam rounded the corner onto 11th Avenue, spun the dinghy to face south, her shoulder-length red hair whipping in the wind, and held her position outside the eight-storey brick building.

'Here we go,' said Jonah, fastening a bright orange life vest around his chest and waist. Sam inspected the buckles and pulled them tight.

'Ow,' said Jonah. 'I need to breathe.'

'There's one more buckle,' she said, nodding at the strap dangling between Jonah's legs. 'But I'll let you do that one.'

Jonah reached down and grabbed the safety strap through his legs, and clipped it up into the triple buckle at his waist.

'Now you won't slip out when it inflates,' Sam said, tossing Jonah an extra life vest as he hoisted himself onto the black iron fire escape.

Jonah clambered up the steep, ladder-like steps. As he rose, he caught a glimpse of 11th Avenue, flooded all the way to downtown. It reminded Jonah of Venice, a city he'd learned about in history class, which had long ago collapsed and succumbed to the sea. When Jonah reached the top floor he crouched down at Jason's window and tapped six times: three quick taps, then two, then just one.

The window opened and the head of Luke Wexler, the world's top video-game designer, leaned out with a smile. But behind the smile, Jonah saw his father.

'Nice of you to drop in, son,' Jason said in Luke's Texan drawl.

'We're *both* going to do the dropping,' said Jonah, handing his father the life vest. Jason stepped out onto the fire escape and buckled up the vest like a pro.

Suddenly, the glass in the window exploded and Jason threw Jonah's head down so hard he tasted the iron grating. He heard the rapid roll of machine-gunfire as he was showered by shards of glass.

'Get down!' called Jason.

Jonah slipped down the fire escape to the seventh floor and Jason followed. The black railing lit up like a sparkler as bullets ricocheted off the iron.

'Come on, Dad!' yelled Jonah, rounding the corner and throwing himself down the next flight of stairs, landing with a painful thump against the railing. Jason followed quickly, sliding down elegantly. The bricks beside Jonah's head burst into red dust. *That was too close*, thought Jonah. It was time to jump.

He motioned to his father to jump into the water below.

As Jonah climbed onto the outer railing, his mind flashed back to one terrible moment, over four months ago, when he had stood at the edge of a much taller building, readying himself to jump into midair, at the same time leaving his mother to perish.

'Pull and jump?' asked Jason, shaking Jonah out of that awful memory.

'No, jump *then* pull,' shouted Jonah as he flung himself into the air and pulled the toggle on the life vest. The vest inflated around him into a bright orange globe, slamming him in the face. He thought he might suffocate as the inflated rubber pressed against his mouth and nose, but before he could fight for another breath, he hit the water hard.

He bounced and rolled, his head submerging into the cold sea water. Jonah struggled with his left arm to pull the deflate cord, but then a bullet penetrated the orange rubber, nullifying his attempts. As the rubber deflated, he saw his father bobbing beside him and swam over to pull his ripcord. Jason soon emerged from his orange ball and the father and son swam to the waiting getaway boat.

Jonah reached up for Sam's hand. It was warm and welcome, pulling Jonah up and over the black military-grade rubber hull. Once he was aboard, both he and Sam hoisted Jason into the dinghy. The water still bubbled with bullets, but Sam gunned the engine urgently and sped them around the corner and back onto 45th Street, out of the line of fire.

It was only then that Jonah took his first full breath of air.

2

Matthew Granger inhaled as he opened the door to the sterile laboratory.

He couldn't help but smile at the familiar, almost comforting scent of antiseptic. It reminded him of his early pioneering days experimenting with Direct Interface, the biochemical technology that linked the human brain to computer servers. Back then he was at the forefront of technology, and full of optimism. He was determined to save the world from itself.

'I found a candidate, sir,' said Rognald, avoiding eye contact with his boss as he thumbed his datapad. Granger peered over the shoulder of the pale and exhausted-looking young bio-hacker and peered into the Metasphere, the global virtual world he had created but now controlled only half of, because of the Guardian terrorists. The Metasphere was the biggest innovation of the twenty-first century, web 4.0: a global virtual world where people could plug in from anywhere on the planet and interface with anyone. Inside the Metasphere, a user appeared as an avatar, the representation of themselves as their subconscious saw them. It was Granger's grand design, combined with his Direct Interface technology, that gave billions of people an alternative to their wretched lives in the overcrowded, polluted and depleted real world. The Metasphere was a second chance for society, but it wasn't just for the living. The Metasphere was also a haven for the dead. The process was called Uploading, and it allowed anyone to Upload their consciousness to the virtual world and live on forever. The process, however, killed the living user. Millions of people had committed suicide to achieve digital immortality.

But ever since Jonah Delacroix, the son of his former private pilot, led the Uploaded into the rival Changsphere virtual world, the dead had grown in consciousness and in determination. Now these Uploaded, hungry for life, roamed Granger's Metasphere, preying on live avatars, usurping them, and logging off in full control of their host's brain and body – reborn in the real world. With his creation under threat, Granger was determined to stop the Uploaded, and Rognald, a bio-hacker whose brilliance was matched only by his own, was his secret weapon.

Granger had rescued Rognald from the slums of Oslo at the age of twelve when the Norwegian prodigy had hacked into Metasphere source code and given hundreds of unsuspecting avatars an extra head. The hack was a prank, punishable by death in most countries, but Granger saw potential in the child and so, as he had done for many of his best Millennials, he arranged a scholarship at a top university in exchange for unwavering loyalty from Rognald. And now Granger had charged him with developing the final solution to the Uploaded, and the prank would be on them.

'Which one?' asked Granger.

'There,' Rognald said, flicking his fingers over the datapad and throwing the image onto the wall. He pointed to a grey squid flying with a bald eagle above a bustling marketplace. 'That's him.'

'He doesn't look like much,' said Granger.

'I've done my homework,' said Rognald, pushing his fine blond hair out of his eyes. 'His name is – was – Sergeant Mark Tarin. U.S. Navy, deceased.'

'How long?'

'He Uploaded eleven years ago at a naval hospital in Virginia, after losing both legs and all motor functions when his helicopter crashed in New York City, I mean…the Republic of Manhattan.'

'The Battle of Central Park?'

'That's the one, sir.'

'And you're sure your virus will fuse to his brainwave patterns?'

'I'm not sure, sir, but I am the most confident about this particular candidate.'

There was no time like the present. The Metasphere was losing users by the second as they had become too fearful to log in, not wanting to risk being usurped and left in the Metasphere whilst someone else logged off and took control of their body. Granger knew the only way to restore faith and trust, and thus control, was to eliminate the Uploaded threat altogether. He needed this final solution.

'Send it in,' instructed Granger.

'Right now?'

'What's stopping you?'

'I haven't fully tested it,' protested Rognald. 'I'd like to run a simulation, then get Tarin in a closed system before introducing the virus.'

'Rognald,' started Granger. 'You're a hacker, and a very good one, but I'm an entrepreneur, and I know that waiting gets you nowhere. We test it fast, and we test *live*.'

'If you really think…'

'I do,' insisted Granger. 'Send in the virus and let's see what happens. If you're right, we know our Extractor is ready. If you're wrong, we move on. Either way, it's progress.'

Rognald drew a circle in the air with his right hand. On-screen, a dotted line grew around the squid and formed a target. 'The virus will latch onto that avatar, fuse with his brainwave patterns and channel his consciousness to our purpose, to…'

'Pull every single Uploaded parasite out of my Metasphere,' Granger said. He reached out and tapped the red button on the datapad.

EXECUTE.

* * *

Andrea Brandon stretched her wings as she flew over the bustling market beside her boyfriend. In the Metasphere, Mark Tarin looked like a sleek grey squid, but when Andrea looked at him, she saw two versions of Mark. She saw the digital avatar, of course; his sleek, oblong face, small blue eyes and flowing tentacles; but at the same time she saw the real-world Mark the way she remembered him, before the crash. She saw the proud and handsome sergeant with a rugged jawbone, tanned skin, close-cropped hair and penetrating blue eyes.

Andrea might have been dead, but she was happy. Uploaded and immortal, she and Mark spent their days soaring above the Metasphere, touching wing to tentacle, marvelling at the beauty of the vast virtual world.

They were together, forever.

Andrea had met Mark in a training simulation at Annapolis, the naval academy, and after they'd fought together in a simulated combat zone, they'd talked, got to know one another and fallen in love. When Manhattan voted for independence, Andrea and Mark flew sorties in the same chopper against the breakaway city-state. But on one covert raid, a rocket launcher shot them out of the night sky and onto the Great Lawn of Central Park.

The twisted metal of the ruined helicopter ripped

through Mark's legs. Andrea fared just as badly, losing her left arm and right leg. They thought they would bleed to death, lying together in the wreckage, hands touching. But the Manhattan rebels arrived and captured them both as prisoners of war. Later, when they were finally traded in a prisoner exchange, they once again lay together in the naval hospital and swore to be together forever. They decided to leave the real world and go to the Island of the Uploaded. Uploading, after all, was forever.

They reached the edge of the marketplace, circled and flew back over it. The avatars below, haggling over digital apps and immersive game files, took every form imaginable. Andrea saw a pair of hippos, giant insects and household pets. Some were mythical beasts – centaurs, goblins, dragons – while others took the forms of robots or machines, and there was even one helicopter. Andrea even spotted a humatar, a rare form of avatar that resembled the user's real-world self. Others were simply abstract shapes. She noticed a green pyramid conclude a trade and fly up towards a glowing golden ring, its exit halo to the real world. The pyramid flew through the circle of light and disappeared. Somewhere on earth, the user behind the pyramid avatar had just opened his or her eyes, sat up from a meta-trance and unplugged from the virtual world.

'Do you want to go down?' she asked, stroking

Mark's tentacles with her outstretched wing.

'I do,' he said in a sad, strained voice, 'but I don't think I should.'

She knew what he meant. Ever since they'd left the Changsphere, they'd become hungry; hungry for life. Had she wanted to, and a dark corner of her soul did want to, she could have usurped that pyramid and woken up in the real world; woken up in someone else's body. But Andrea and Mark prided themselves on their military discipline; they wouldn't give in to the basest of human greed. They refused to steal another person's life.

'We can just keep soaring, then,' she said, as if nothing were wrong. 'I like it up here.'

'It's just safer,' he sighed.

It's just safer, she repeated to herself.

A sudden blast-wave sent Andrea and Mark reeling backwards as it rocked the marketplace below. As they regained their balance, they spotted a mysterious orange orb materialising in the middle of the market. It pulsed and glowed unlike any avatar Andrea had ever seen, and yet it had eyes. And it was looking right at Andrea.

The orb pulsed and shot up into the air, heading straight for the couple above.

'What is th—' Mark's words were cut off as the orb completely enveloped him.

'Mark!' Andrea shouted as she desperately tried to

pry the orange attacker off her soul mate. But the orb had surrounded him and he was trapped inside. The orb seemed to fuse with Mark's grey, shimmering skin, dyeing him orange. When he opened his eyes, they were no longer blue, but black, reflective and lifeless.

'Mark, what happened to—'

'An-dre-a,' Mark stuttered. 'Get. Out. Of. Here.'

One of Mark's now orange tentacles shot out towards Andrea but Mark grabbed it with another, and pulled it back. In that instant, Andrea saw something terrifying at the tip of it.

She saw a mouth.

Andrea flapped her wings and shot into the sky. Mark still struggled with himself, holding back his tentacles from reaching her, but three of his tentacles shot out below, stretching impossibly far to chase three separate avatars in the marketplace.

The first tentacle constricted around a horrified crocodile. The second ensnared a fleeing mantis, and the third plucked a screaming sunflower out of the air. The tips of the tentacles then opened up and the air was filled with a deafening whirling sound.

Above, Andrea covered her white head with her black wings to block out the terrible noise, but she could still see the three avatars as they were sucked right into Mark's hungry appendages.

Two of the captured avatars, the mantis and the

flower, were replaced by completely new avatars. The mantis had been replaced by a trembling white poodle that drifted slowly to the ground, blinking in the sunlight. And a jittery housefly now buzzed where the flower had just been flying. Strangely, Andrea noticed that the crocodile had simply disappeared, not replaced by anything or anyone.

But as she looked at Mark, at the monster he'd become, a familiar avatar finally materialised beside him. A black spider.

It was Matthew Granger.

'There is no need to be alarmed,' said the spider in a calm, confident voice. 'The Millennials have a solution for the scourge of the Uploaded. You have all witnessed the first deployment of our Extractor virus. This virus will not only seek out the Uploaded that have already usurped innocent avatars, but also target those who yearn to usurp you. It is time for immortality to end. The Extractor will purge the Uploaded from our Metasphere.'

The crowd below cheered.

Purge.

The word rang out in Andrea's head.

The spider nodded to the shaking fly and then turned back to address the crowd. 'Spread the good word: my Millennials will not rest until the Metasphere is safe for the living.'

The spider stepped into his glowing exit halo and

disappeared, leaving the mutated Mark Tarin, now an orange squid with hungry tentacles, scanning the crowd, searching for more Uploaded to extract. He locked eyes with Andrea, and for the first time in a long, long time, she felt something stronger than hunger.

She felt fear.

3

The black dinghy bolted down Broadway.

Water sprayed Jonah in the face as the threesome approached the glaring colours and buzzing billboards of Times Square.

'Thank you, both of you, for getting me out,' said Jason.

'We're not out yet!' shouted Sam.

'Axel and the others are waiting on the barge,' explained Jonah to his dad. 'Off the Lower East Side.'

'So we've got to get off the island before the water is pumped out,' said Sam.

'Or the police catch us,' added Jason, nervously looking up at the digital news ticker.

Jonah glanced upwards at the screens. They had finally caught up with the chaos below. Rolling text warned residents to stay indoors and keep to the upper levels. One screen showed footage of a strange, orange squid in the Metasphere with the headline 'MILLENNIAL SAVIOUR', while another displayed blurry images of Floridian pirate boats with the news ticker reading 'HOSTAGE CRISIS OFF MIAMI.'

'Looks like our jailbreak hasn't made the news yet,' said Jonah, breathing a sigh of relief.

'It won't be long,' said Sam.

'Unless the Co-op covers it up,' said Jason. 'Letting me escape with Luke's body wouldn't look so good come re-election time.'

Up ahead, in the middle of the flooded Times Square, Jonah spotted a pile-up of yellow auto-cabs. *That should have been impossible*, he thought. Manhattan's traffic was controlled by a smart grid system. *The flood must have shorted something out,* thought Jonah, *or confused the system's sensors.* He counted four – no, five – yellow auto-cabs, all tangled up with each other. The front wheels of one cab were buried in the roof of another. Jonah couldn't see anyone inside the cabs, which was a mercy.

But then, as they got closer, he noticed another upturned vehicle stuck among the wreckage. A gleaming black SUV, flipped over, wheels up – like a helpless turtle. A man in a drenched black suit clung to the exposed axle of the vehicle. His face was bleeding and he struggled for breath. The SUV was partially supported by the wreckage of the cabs but it was slipping and sliding down into the water.

Jonah watched the SUV's licence plate sinking beneath the surface: PREXY 1.

The president's car. Lori Weisberg's car!

Lori was the young president of Manhattan, barely older than Jonah, who'd helped Jonah and Sam break into One World Trade Center to rescue Jason from

Granger. She was a good leader and she didn't deserve to die this way. She was also the first girl Jonah had ever kissed.

'Slow down, Sam,' Jonah called as he spotted another man, soaking wet in a ripped black suit, crawling on top of the stricken vehicle.

'Not on your life,' she shouted back. 'We've got to get out of here.'

As they sailed past the pile-up Jonah locked eyes with the first suited man and, although he couldn't hear what he said, Jonah read his lips: 'She's trapped!'

Jonah shuffled back in the dinghy and put his hand on Sam's, on top of the tiller.

'Please, it's Lori. I can't let her drown.'

'Jason, this is the woman who locked you up,' called Sam, hoping for his support. 'And she'll do it again if you get caught.'

'I'm with Jonah on this,' he said. 'We can't just let her die.'

Sam shook her head. 'What is it with you Delacroixes?'

'*Sam*,' pleaded Jonah. 'Do it for me.'

'Whenever I do something for you, it leads to a world of trouble,' she said, exhaling with resignation.

She pulled the tiller hard to the right, circling the dinghy to the port side, and doubling back to moor alongside the overturned wreck. She cut the motor and nuzzled the boat beside the sinking

26

SUV. Jonah steadied himself to dive.

'Wait!' shouted Sam, shrugging off her rucksack and unthreading the straps. 'That car's more heavily armoured than your average tank. You're gonna need something a bit more explosive to get you into it.'

From her rucksack, which also contained a variety of tools and a gun, Sam passed Jonah a tiny blob of plastique, just a few grams, and a blasting cap with a detonator cord. Jonah helped himself to Sam's knife from her life vest pocket.

'Thank you,' he said before jumping from the dinghy onto the bottom of the upturned SUV. The car groaned and shifted beneath his sudden weight and Jonah held onto a rear tyre until it had had settled again. Jonah guessed that its roof had come to rest on the street below.

He peered down over the rear axle of the car. He could make out the shape of the SUV's hatchback in the murky water. Through the window he could see a familiar face, and he felt his stomach tightening. Lori!

The water was filling the SUV, reaching up to the floor. The teenage president strained at the surface, gasping for her last breaths.

Jonah jumped into the water and pulled on the door. But the security system that was designed to keep Lori safe inside now trapped her in a watery death cage.

Sam was right. 'We need to blow it!' he called out.

Jonah could see Lori was now holding her breath,

her cheeks puffed out as she hammered hopelessly on the reinforced glass with her fists.

She had no air left.

Then she saw Jonah, and her desperate eyes widened with hope.

He motioned to Lori to get back, showing her the plastique. She seemed to understand, because she pushed herself away from the rear window.

Jonah didn't have much time. How long could she hold her breath for?

He willed his hands not to tremble as he moulded the plastique around the hatch's lock. Then he scrambled back along the SUV and set off the blasting cap.

Jonah was sprayed with water. The explosion was only a small one, but it worked. The hatch had blown open, and Jonah dived down and swam in through the rear of the SUV. He grabbed Lori's limp body and hauled her out, pushing against the vehicle with his feet before he ran out of oxygen.

When he surfaced, clutching Lori with one arm, Jason jumped from the dinghy and grabbed her lifeless body. Together they hoisted the unconscious president up onto the undercarriage. Jason tilted Lori's head back, opening up her airway. Jonah had never learned CPR, but his dad's memories were still imprinted in his brain from the time he had spent cloaked in Jason's avatar. He knew instinctively what to do: *ABC* – airway, breathing, circulation.

'I'll do breaths, you compress,' Jonah said, his father instantly understanding the plan.

Jonah leaned down and placed his mouth on Lori's. He gave her two quick rescue breaths. Jason pumped down hard on her chest, trying to jump-start her heart. Father and son operated in synch, giving her breath and circulation and bringing her back from the brink of death.

Jonah moved his mouth away as Lori gasped, coughed and spluttered. She turned her head, spitting out water, and then looked up at Jonah, clearly scared but also confused.

'Y-you?!' she sputtered. Lori pointed at Jason and addressed her two exhausted bodyguards. 'Arrest the body snatcher!'

BANG!

The shot rang out throughout Times Square. Jonah looked over to see Sam lower her gun from the skyward warning to point it straight at Lori's head. Jonah knew Sam was an ace shot; she wouldn't miss.

'The only people allowed to move are both named Delacroix,' she called. 'Into this boat.'

Lori looked at her men and subtly shook her head, warning them to keep their weapons holstered.

'I can't let you take that body,' said Lori as Jason slid from the SUV and into the black dinghy.

'I'm sorry,' said Jonah. 'But I can't let you keep him. You know it's not safe for him here.'

As he lowered himself to follow Jason, Lori put her hands on his left arm and said, 'Thank you.' A flicker of decision crossing her face, she leaned in and kissed Jonah on the lips. Her wet hair dripped over Jonah's face and he froze for what felt like an hour. The last time Lori had kissed him, Jonah had been about to zip-line into a warzone. He realised he liked being kissed by her, but wished it didn't have to come with risking his life. 'That's for saving me,' she added, as she pulled her lips from his. And then she slapped him.

'And that's for everything else,' she said with presidential composure. 'Until you return that body to its rightful owner, all three of you are enemies of the state.'

'Let's go, lover-boy,' chided Sam, keeping the gun trained on Lori's head.

Jonah moved into the dinghy, trying to shake off the shock of what had just happened. He was overwhelmed with relief that he had been able to save Lori, but disappointed that he could never return to Manhattan.

With one hand still holding her gun, Sam revved the engine and sped south down Broadway, away from the lights, away from the crash, and away from Jonah's first crush.

He didn't look back.

4

Granger stared at the three avatars projected on the wall of the laboratory: a crocodile, a mantis and a sunflower.

'It worked, sir,' sighed Rognald with relief, stroking the pale facial hair over his jaw line.

'No it didn't,' corrected Granger. 'It missed one.' He grabbed Rognald's datapad and pulled up the virus's report, throwing it onto the wall. 'The Extractor identified four Uploaded in its range, and only grabbed three. Why?'

The report showed the three captured Uploaded, plus the escaped eagle.

'I don't understand,' admitted the bio-hacker. 'It just didn't grab the eagle.'

'I won't tolerate a twenty-five percent failure rate.'

'And you shouldn't have to,' said Rognald, taking back his datapad and adjusting the settings. 'I'll boost the processing power.'

On screen, the orange squid fluttered and pulsed as more power surged into it.

'Let's steer it somewhere a bit more…populated,' suggested Granger. Of course, he knew the young hacker understood that a *suggestion* and an *order* were the same thing. 'I want an ops team to follow it in-world, and direct it to the known Uploaded hideouts. Who's online now and ready to deploy?'

'Sander's team are live,' said Rognald.

'He'll have to do,' grunted Granger, tapping the green CALL icon on his own datapad screen and scrolling through avatars until he reached the icon of a smiling blond humatar.

The humatar appeared on screen, flanked by a fox and a large tree. 'Mr Granger,' he said, 'this is an unexpected honour. What can I do for you?'

'Sander, I've deployed the Extractor virus in the Metasphere. Rognald is sending you its coordinates, and I want you and your team to lead it to the Uploaded.'

'And then what?'

'Let it loose,' said Granger.

'With pleasure,' said Sander.

Granger drew his thumb and forefinger together like a tiny pincer on the datapad, closing the meta-window between the virtual world and the real world, and strode out of the white lab. He marched down a narrow steel corridor, climbed a steep flight of metal stairs and emerged onto the long, flat deck of a massive, steel-hulled boat.

The *Marin Avenger*.

The *Avenger* was a repurposed oil tanker, fitted with large, billowing sails. But it also had powerful engines, which ran on an efficient biofuel blend. A tall metal structure rose from the stern end of the deck: an airship-docking tower. A huge grey dirigible floated over the deck, attached to the tower by its nose.

Granger had bought the *Marin Avenger* when he was fifteen, with the proceeds from his first patents. For two months now – since he was exiled from Manhattan – it had served as his mobile Command Headquarters.

It was from the deck of this great boat that Granger planned to save the world. *His* world. His Metasphere. A world that he created, at the age of nineteen – two decades ago – from nothing but imagination and programming code.

His Metasphere.

Granger would save the Metasphere from the threat of the Uploaded, and then he would be free to turn his attention to the Guardians, a global group of anarchists and terrorists that had seized control of half of his Metasphere and transformed it into a lawless outland.

He would purge the world of the Guardians.

Jonah climbed the rope ladder onto the Guardian sail barge. His father followed, with Sam securing the dinghy to two hoisting ropes below. Once Jonah was over the railing, he reached down and helped his dad aboard.

The barge looked ancient and decrepit, but the Guardians had retrofitted it with powerful biofuel engines that could handle any load with ease. Once, a long time ago, the barge had transported coal. Now, its huge, flat deck – bigger than two football pitches laid end to end – was piled chest-high with grey metal boxes.

The boxes were swathed in green tarpaulin and old, thick ropes. The weather was dry, for now, but there was a likelihood of rainstorms further south, so the barge's precious cargo had to be protected.

Each metal box held a cluster of fully networked micro-servers, each of them about the size of a personal hard drive: the very latest in technology, and the most vital component of the Guardians' plan to transfer the data from the Eastern Corner and distribute it across the world. The Guardians had already secured the Southern Corner in Australia and the Western Corner in Manhattan, and now it was time to tip the balance of this metawar to their side by taking the Eastern Corner.

Red and brown sails billowed over the deck. The barge could run on biofuel, but Jonah guessed its captain favoured the free power of wind when it was available.

'Where's my little girl?' bellowed a voice from across the deck. Jonah looked over to see Axel, Sam's father, striding towards them. Axel had broad shoulders, flowing grey hair and an infectious laugh. He pulled Sam up and embraced her in a big bear hug.

'Hiya, Dad,' said Sam, squirming out of the hug. Jonah felt a pang of jealousy as he watched Sam and her father embrace. He was happy to have his own dad back, but knew that as long as Jason inhabited a stolen body, he was never truly back for good.

Axel turned to Jason with an outstretched hand.

'It's good to have you back, partner,' he said. 'The kids did well, didn't they?'

'They sure did,' said Jason, roughly ruffling Jonah's hair. 'They must've learned something from us.'

'Da-ad,' complained Jonah, trying in vain to slick down his unruly black tufts.

'It was Axel who used the tidal power system to flood the city,' explained Sam.

'Used their own infrastructure against them,' boasted Axel. 'Oldest trick in the book.'

'I'm just glad you got me out,' said Jason. 'That apartment started as a prison to keep me in, but when Bryony leaked the address, it turned into a safe house to keep out the lynch mobs.'

'Fear will do that,' said Axel. 'People are afraid of...' Jonah could tell he stopped himself saying 'you'.

'Most of the Uploaded can't control their hunger,' Jonah began. 'They're either hiding out, staying away from the living, or—'

'Usurping them,' said Sam. 'Which reminds me, Jonah, we're overdue for patrol.'

'What patrol?' asked Jason.

'We're working on a cure for the Uploaded's hunger, Jason,' explained Axel, 'but until we do, we're tracking them and putting them somewhere safe.'

'Safe for whom?' asked Jason.

Jonah didn't like the direction this was going. He could tell in his father's voice, even through Luke's Texan accent, that he wasn't comfortable targeting the Uploaded.

'It's for everyone's protection,' Jonah tried to explain. 'And Sam's right, we're due in the Metasphere.'

'And we have prep work for the Eastern Corner campaign,' said Axel, gripping Jason's shoulder.

'Are we going to make it all the way to *Iraq* in this bucket of bolts?' asked Jason.

'No need. Granger's moved the Eastern Corner,' said Jonah. 'At least temporarily.'

'To where?'

'The one place no one wants to go,' said Axel. 'Cuba.'

'Is it safe?' asked Jason. 'I mean, the radiation must be—'

'Don't forget, you've been dead for three years,' said Axel. 'The radiation levels have depleted, but I'm not rushing to buy beach-front if you know what I mean.'

Jonah remembered the metacast of the Guantanamo Bay explosion, the nuclear bomb that hit Cuba during its civil war, but he couldn't tell if the memory was his or his father's.

'So long as we don't stay for more than twenty-four hours, we'll be fine,' explained Sam.

'How did we find the servers if Granger moved them?' asked Jason.

'Jez has an informer inside the Millennials,' said Axel.

Jonah had never liked Jez, and wasn't sure he could trust him. But he had fought, and been wounded, in the underground battle for the Western Corner in Manhattan, which was more than Jonah could boast.

'Let's get to work, people,' commanded Axel. 'We make landfall in twenty-three hours.'

Jonah turned to follow Sam to a DI port, but Jason grabbed him. 'A minute?'

'Yeah, Dad, of course.'

Jonah and Jason stepped up and onto the metal gangway above the hundreds of micro-servers.

'You don't have to do this,' Jason said.

'What?'

'Any of it. Fighting the Millennials. Saving the Metasphere. This was my life; I should have never dragged you into it.'

'Dad, if we don't stop the Uploaded, there won't be a Metasphere worth saving,' said Jonah. He felt so conflicted by the rise of the Uploaded. On one hand, he was so happy to have his father back in the real world, even in someone else's body. On the other hand, Jonah knew that as long as the Uploaded roamed the Metasphere, hunting for life, the virtual world would become as derelict as the real world.

'They're lucky to have you,' said Jason. 'I'm lucky to have you.'

'Thanks, Dad,' said Jonah, eyeing Sam waiting impatiently. 'I gotta go.' Jason pulled Jonah into a hug, and held him tight.

When Jason finally released his son, Sam and Jonah walked to the aft of the boat, and Jonah watched the skyline of Manhattan receding into the distance, the sun dipping behind the skyscrapers.

'I guess we won't be holidaying in Manhattan any time soon,' she joked.

'No,' sighed Jonah, 'I guess we won't.'

'No second thoughts about leaving your girlfriend behind?'

'She isn't my girlfriend,' he said defensively. He *had* begun to think of Lori as a friend, but, despite saving her life, he was sure she'd never forgive him for flooding her city and busting out Jason. He hoped she wouldn't face a coup by her Board.

'Don't worry about her,' said Sam. She seemed to have a talent for always knowing what Jonah was thinking. 'The flood water will have drained away by now. There'll be a lot of mopping up to be done, but no lasting harm.'

Jonah nodded, and tore his gaze away from the shrinking skyscrapers on the horizon. *No point dwelling on the past,* he told himself. *You have the future to think about.*

5

Jonah and Sam were going to hunt tigers at the circus.

While their real-world bodies were meta-tranced in their hammocks aboard the Guardian barge, Jonah and Sam slipped into the Metasphere for patrol duty. They were responding to the sighting of an Uploaded.

As always, after connecting the DI cable to the socket in his lower back and tapping in his Point of Origin coordinates, the transition between worlds made Jonah feel dizzy and a little nauseous. But he was glad to be back in the Metasphere. It felt like coming home.

In the virtual world, Jonah's avatar was a *humatar*, a digital doppelgänger of his gangly real-world self; a pixel-formed personification that even captured his unruly dark hair. In contrast, Sam appeared as a sleek, pearly-white unicorn, her mane the same shade of red as Sam's real-world hair, with a pair of white wings sprouting from her back.

Jonah felt a pang of jealousy as she extended her wings. When Jonah had filtered his father's dragon avatar, he'd relished the power that came with his mighty wings, and still missed them even though he could fly without them.

They flew along past the sideshows, weaving between jugglers, fire-breathers and sword-swallowers. The acts seemed old-fashioned and trivial to Jonah, although he had enjoyed them once, many years before, with his mum and dad. But the circus had changed since then. Or maybe it was Jonah who'd changed, he realised.

They touched down, hovering between the low-res tents and blocky booths. The entire area felt in dire need of an upgrade, especially compared to the immersive games that dominated the Metasphere's entertainment scene. Jonah noticed an area of corrupted code, a mash-up of pixels with grey patches seeping through, cordoned off by electronic caution tape.

Jonah heard a horn tooting, and leapt out of the way of a yellow clown car. Its white-faced occupant was hunched over the steering wheel, scowling. He had almost run into Jonah without seeing him. A goldfish avatar called out to Jonah from a ring-toss booth, but her sales pitch was flat and uninviting.

Visitors to the circus were well outnumbered by performers, and a subdued, melancholy atmosphere hung over the whole place. The circus was in one of the oldest sectors of the Metasphere, and had long since been supplanted by more spectacular sights and more exciting experiences elsewhere. Of course now, even those attractions were just as desolate. The entire

Metasphere was haunted by the Uploaded, turning many non-essential sectors into ghost towns. Some users felt forced to brave the Metasphere for financial reasons, while others simply believed that usurping would never happen to them. But more and more users stayed off-line for fear of being taken over by the dead.

Jonah and Sam were part of a globally coordinated Guardian mission to make the Metasphere safe again.

For the past two months, while Axel and the Guardians cleared out the Western Corner servers beneath Manhattan, Jonah and Sam had joined a network of Guardians that patrolled the Metasphere for the roaming Uploaded. There was still no cure for their hunger. Yet. But the Guardians, who now controlled half of the virtual world, and had their sights on the other half, were working feverishly on a cure. Erel Dias, the brilliant Millennial defector who had programmed the protocol that could separate a willing Uploaded from its living host, was leading the Guardian scientists in desperate pursuit of a cure. Until then, Guardian patrols rounded up the Uploaded, captured them using a newly created digital lasso, and sent them to a quarantined camp in the Metasphere where they could be kept separate from the living.

Jonah had logged seventy-nine missions and

captured two hundred and twenty-eight Uploaded since joining the patrol. Today, he'd been called in to confront two identical tigers; he was looking forward to reaching two hundred and thirty.

Their destination, the big top, was closed. A red and white 'no entry' icon flashed over the entrance. But Jonah could hear music playing inside the tent.

He pushed aside the tent flap and he and Sam floated past the empty ticket booth. They continued along the edge of the tiered audience seating. The music was louder now, all brass and drum rolls and cymbal clashes, although with no obvious source.

Two massive Bengal tigers, one slightly bigger than the other, were performing above the circus ring for a packed audience of no one.

The big cats wove through an obstacle course of burning hoops. The hoops were spinning around the circus ring, swapping places, but the tigers' reflexes and agility were incredible. They twisted and turned their lithe bodies in midair to swoop through each hoop in turn, never once touching the flames.

'They're incredible,' gasped Jonah.

'They're incredibly dangerous,' said Sam.

She was right. If the tigers were Uploaded, they could attack the living at any moment. For Jonah, whose father not only was Uploaded, but had also usurped the body of a living avatar, hunting them was something he knew was right, but hated doing. It was just a matter of time before a hunting party would be sent to capture his dad.

'You don't look like paying customers,' barked a raspy voice.

An avatar drifted down from the stands. It – *he*, from the voice – was a tall top hat, patterned with silver and blue stars.

'We're Guardians,' said Sam. 'We got a pop-up about the Uploaded.'

'Took you long enough,' complained the top hat.

'Are you the ringmaster?' asked Jonah.

'What gave it away?' the hat huffed. *Of course he was*, Jonah thought. He wondered which had come first. Had the ringmaster got this job because he looked the part – or did he look the part because, deep down, this was what he had always seen himself doing? It was said, after all, that the form of a person's avatar expressed his or her truest self.

'I'm Samantha Kavanaugh and this is Jonah Delacroix. What can you tell us about them?' asked Sam, pointing to the leaping tigers.

'They just wandered in here in the middle of a show, three days ago, and won't leave. They insist on performing, even when there's no one to see them. We had to clear the tent, of course. We couldn't take the risk that they'd usurp someone.'

'Are you sure they're Uploaded?' asked Jonah.

'The big one calls himself the Dazzling D'Iferno,'

said the ringmaster, the whole hat nodding. 'And she calls herself Amaza. They claim that, in the real world, they were the greatest acrobatic double act in the world. And you know what? I actually saw them perform when I was a little boy. They were dazzling. And amazing.'

Jonah flexed his wrist, and a small icon appeared in front of him: an iron safe, which only he could see. His inventory space. He reached in and pulled out a coiled length of rope: a lasso. Another flick of the wrist, and the loop of the lasso began to glow red. The rope's glowing loop looked like an exit halo. If it passed over its target, it would have a similar effect. The technology had been programmed by Dias and worked on any Uploaded avatar, but only on the Uploaded – those who no longer had their own bodies in the real world.

Jonah stepped forward into the circus ring. 'We'll take it from here.'

Sam kept close by Jonah's side, unfurling her own glowing lasso.

'Mr D'Iferno, Ms Amaza,' Jonah shouted. 'I'm sorry but you can't be here.'

But the twin tigers ignored him. D'Iferno tucked his legs into his stomach, dropped and barrel-rolled through three burning hoops in the split second that all three were aligned. Amaza followed in perfect symmetry.

'You're scaring off my customers!' the ringmaster

pleaded. 'It's hard enough to get people through the gates these days, without—'

'Go away!' the larger tiger growled.

'Can't you see we're performing?' purred Amaza.

Sam and Jonah moved around the circus ring in opposite directions, watching for an opening, lassoes at the ready.

'We can't do that,' said Sam. 'This quarter of the Metasphere is run by the Guardians now, and the users are afraid—'

'Guardians, Millennials!' D'Iferno spat. 'I don't care about your turf war. I just want to perform. It's the only way to keep the hunger at bay!'

'We're so *hungry*,' said Amaza.

'We're working on a cure for that,' said Jonah. 'But until we can find it—'

'Promises, always promises!'

'Until we find a cure,' said Sam, stalling for time until she and Jonah could pounce, 'it's best we keep the Uploaded and the living separated. It's for your own good as much as ours. We've created a safe place—'

'Safe for whom?' shouted D'Iferno as he swooped down at Sam, his claws out, his teeth bared. Sam dived out of the tiger's way, throwing her lasso at the same time. But to the Dazzling D'Iferno, it was just another burning hoop. He avoided it with casual ease.

'Brother, don't!' called Amaza. But D'Iferno wasn't listening. The big cat was now sprawled on top of Sam and batting her back and forth like an oversized mouse.

'Sam!' shouted Jonah as he flew across the ring towards her. He threw his lasso ahead of him with a fierce whip-crack motion, but D'Iferno dodged it as if he had eyes in the back of his head, jumping off Sam momentarily to save himself.

Jonah sailed past his target and the tiger pounced on Sam again. Before she could swing her lasso, D'Iferno knocked it out of her hoof and pushed the stumbling unicorn back against the stands. Sam struggled furiously, but she was pinned by the ferocious tiger.

Jonah hurled himself onto D'Iferno, and unravelled his own lasso to strike. But suddenly he was knocked sideways by Amaza.

'Get off my brother,' she called. 'You just couldn't leave us alone, could you?'

D'Iferno snarled, right up in Sam's face. 'I told you, performing these old tricks is what keeps the hunger in check. But since you insist on interrupting me, we should just give in to it and do what the others do. What do they call it now? *Slurping*?'

'Usurping,' said Amaza. 'But brother, it's... it's *wrong*.'

D'Iferno opened his jaws. 'But it feels so right,

sister,' he said. 'And there's one for each of us. A double act.'

'D'Iferno, no!' cried Jonah, fumbling with his tangled lasso.

'How I'd give anything to perform in the real world again,' D'Iferno purred, salivating.

'You can't have my body,' Sam gasped, still straining to push the tiger away from her. 'I won't let you...'

But D'Iferno threw open his jaws – and they kept on stretching to an impossible width, until his mouth was bigger than Sam's head, and then the whole of her unicorn's body.

The tiger lunged at Sam, and clamped his jaws shut around her.

Jonah finally untangled his lasso. He flew at the Dazzling D'Iferno again, terrified that he might be too late, that he might lose Sam forever.

'Get off her!' he yelled.

The tiger began to turn, but in that moment of feasting he was sluggish, his reactions slowed. Jonah stretched out the glowing red loop of his lasso and slammed it down over D'Iferno's head all the way to the sandy floor.

The tiger disappeared and crouching in his place inside the red ring, trembling and shaken, was Sam's pearly-white unicorn.

Jonah fell to his knees, threw his arms around Sam

and buried his face deep in her red mane. 'I was afraid...I thought I'd lost you!'

A horrible thought occurred to him. He pulled away and looked into Sam's eyes. 'You are still...?' he started. 'I mean, it is still you in there?'

Sam nodded, smiling bravely. 'You got to me just in time, Jonah. I could feel him inside my head. I could feel his memories rushing in to replace my own. For a second, just a second, I almost thought I *was* him. I could feel his hunger. Jonah, it was so strong.'

'It's OK, Sam. You're OK. He's gone now.'

'Brother?' cried Amaza. 'What have you done with him?'

Sam got to her feet and gave her body a shake. Jonah moved to place himself between Sam and Amaza. Jonah was immune to usurping; he would rather grapple with the big cat than put Sam at risk again. 'I sent him away, to the Camp.'

The tigress looked confused, and Jonah explained, 'The Camp is a safe place, a specially coded island.'

'Like the old Island of the Uploaded,' Sam added.

'The Island was a sanctuary,' Amaza hissed. 'You sent him to a prison!'

'No,' protested Sam, keeping her distance from the angry beast. 'We're gathering the Uploaded there so that when there's a cure for your hunger—'

'But I haven't usurped anyone.'

'Not yet,' said Jonah. 'But believe me, sooner or

later the hunger will become too strong. It will overtake you and you won't be able to stop yourself. It happens to the…' Jonah stopped himself, thinking of his father. 'To the best of you.'

'Then you'll have to catch me first,' she said, sprinting out of the big top.

'There she goes,' sighed Sam.

'Are you sure you're up for this?' he asked.

Sam spread her wings and soared into the air. 'It's just no fun if they don't run.'

'Let's go and get her,' Jonah shouted after her, leaping up and flying out of the big top.

6

Andrea soared over the beach and touched down amid a crowd of avatars that she knew were fellow Uploaded. She saw two seals laughing in the water, a family of otters body-surfing the waves, and a group of hexagons gossiping around a virtual bonfire.

This long stretch of beach reminded many of the Uploaded of their original Island, and was known among the Uploaded as a safe haven, a place where no living avatar dared to come, and thus a place free from the temptation to take life. Andrea and Mark had spent many a happy afternoon wading in the waves, but now she was here to warn the others of the horrors she'd witnessed.

'The living have unleashed something terrible,' she said, trying to get the attention of the sun worshippers. 'It took my Mark, it changed him, and now he – *it* – is hunting us, hunting the Uploaded.'

But her warning fell on deaf ears. The Uploaded paid no attention to Andrea. They simply wanted to bask in their sun-soaked ignorance. They just wanted to enjoy themselves.

Jonah and Sam pursued Amaza across the Metasphere

and eventually over a massive body of water.

'Sam, let's turn back,' Jonah called. 'She's taking us too far from our halos.'

With Sam and Jonah's exit halos, their portals back to the real world, hovering at the circus, they couldn't make a quick getaway from the Metasphere if they were attacked by the Uploaded. Jonah wasn't worried about himself; he could stand up against any intruder into his brain, but he wished Sam wasn't so cavalier about pushing deep into the Metasphere to bag her prey.

'I'm not letting her get away,' she said, narrowing the gap with the fleeing tigress.

In response, Jonah put his arms straight out to each side and focused on speed; he wasn't going to let Sam out of his reach again.

Amaza banked to the left, and Jonah spotted a long stretch of beach below.

'There!' called Jonah. 'When she touches down, push her towards me and I'll lasso her.'

Jonah pulled his glowing red lasso out of his inventory space as he landed on the warm, sandy beach. A sudden gasp from the sunbathers alerted Jonah to the fact that this beach was a refuge for the Uploaded.

'A Guardian lasso,' someone shouted.

'Patrol!'

'They're here to take us to the Camp,' rang out

another frightened voice.

Jonah didn't know if Amaza had deliberately led them into a trap – a place where Jonah couldn't possibly protect Sam against thirty or more Uploaded – or if she had simply fled to the only place she could think of. Either way, they were here and they were outnumbered.

'I need to you come with me,' said Sam, approaching Amaza. The tigress retreated from Sam's red lasso, walking backwards towards Jonah. One more step and Jonah could nab her. He readied his lasso to encircle the fugitive tigress.

But he wasn't quick enough. At the same moment, an orange snake shot from the sky and devoured Amaza in one gulp.

'What on Earth...?' asked Jonah. But before he could finish his thought, the sky was suddenly filled with orange snakes, all pouncing on the Uploaded.

The sunbathing Uploaded scattered, but they didn't stand a chance.

One by one, the strange serpents began sucking the Uploaded away. There was nothing Sam and Jonah could do. It was only when Jonah looked up that he saw the snakes were actually tentacles belonging to one huge single avatar. The orange squid was sucking up the Uploaded with cruel efficiency.

'Margaret!' Jonah heard someone call. He looked over at a black seal in the water, calling out to another smaller seal on the sand. The orange tentacle sucked up the smaller seal as she struggled along the beach.

'Jonah, what *is* that?' asked Sam, rushing to his side.

'I don't know, but it's taking them all,' said Jonah, looking back at the seal emerging from the water. Jonah shouted to him: 'Stay under, hide under the water!'

The seal ducked just in time. A tentacle reached down and thrashed about in the water, but it couldn't track the seal under the digital waves.

Above Jonah's head, he spotted a bald eagle evading another tentacle. The eagle flew in a zigzag before following the seal's lead: dive-bombing into the water and disappearing.

'Amazing, isn't it?' asked a voice from behind them. Jonah turned around to see a trio of avatars: a humatar, a fox and a large tree.

'This is Millennial innovation, keeping you safe,' said the blond humatar.

Jonah looked up and down the beach. It was desolate, stripped bare of the Uploaded. Jonah, Sam and the three newcomers were all that remained, standing in the sandy shadow of the hovering squid.

'Where did that thing take them?' asked Jonah.

'Somewhere they can't hurt you,' boasted the fox.

'Sander,' whispered the tree in a low voice, prodding

the humatar with a branch. The tree was trying to get the humatar's attention, but Sander seemed more interested in showing off his technology.

'This is Millennial innovation, keeping you safe,' repeated Sander with a salesmanlike smile.

'I don't think they were hurting anyone,' protested Jonah. 'They were just gathered here, far from any living avatar, just—'

'Just waiting for the hunger to overtake them,' said Sander. 'They might have been peaceful sunbathers today, but tomorrow they could have tried to usurp you, or your pretty unicorn girlfriend.'

'She's not my—'

'This pretty unicorn could deconstruct you in one hack,' said Sam.

'Whoa nellie,' said Sander. 'We don't want any trouble, we're just keeping the Metasphere safe for the living.'

'Sander,' boomed the tree in a low, bass voice. 'That's J.D., and that's the Kavanaugh girl.'

'Guardians,' snarled the fox, baring her teeth.

'And this is our quarter of the Metasphere,' said Sam.

'If you want it "free and open",' mocked Sander, 'you gotta live with whomever wanders in.'

'Where did that thing send the Uploaded?' asked Jonah, changing the subject.

Sander laughed. 'Like I'd tell you. Just be glad it

isn't programmed to suck up Guardians, though that'd be a good upgrade.'

Sander and the others two Millennials flew up to the squid and pulled it away on a lead, like a child with a helium balloon.

'Sam,' began Jonah. 'The Uploaded aren't safe in here with that thing roaming around.'

'And the living aren't safe in here with the Uploaded roaming around,' she said.

'But this'll escalate the tension between the living and dead,' Jonah concluded.

'It's inevitable,' said Sam. 'No one can be immortal, but everyone wants to be.'

'We have to warn the Camp,' said Jonah, taking to the sky. 'If that thing finds it…'

He couldn't finish the thought. He didn't need to. Sam rose to his side and the two flew towards the Guardians' quarantine camp.

The eagle, Andrea, emerged from the water to see the humatar and unicorn fly away.

She flapped her wings dry and flew to the empty beach. Everyone was gone. All of those helpless avatars had been simply sucked away. They were peaceful Uploaded who refused to give in to the hunger and had chosen to stay apart from the living. But the living had come looking for them, had hunted them.

'Margaret, Margaret!' called someone from the

water. It was the black seal, awkwardly surfacing from the waves. 'My darling Margaret, where are you?'

'They're all gone,' Andrea said in disbelief. 'Every single one of them.'

'But my wife,' said the seal in an old man's voice. 'She's – she's all I have in this world.'

'They took her.'

'Who?' trembled the seal.

'The living.'

The seal shuddered, and Andrea put her wing on his slippery back, consoling the man as he cried. 'I'm so sorry,' she said. 'I…I lost someone too,' she confessed – without revealing that it was her boyfriend, Mark, who'd been turned into the orange squid monster that ripped the Uploaded from the Metasphere.

'We've been together for seventy-five years,' he sobbed. 'Fifty-seven in the real world, and the rest in here. We shared an Uploading ceremony. We were supposed to be together forever. We were supposed to be immortal.'

'I know, I know.'

'Someone needs to do something,' he said. 'Someone needs to fight back. The living are scared of us, and they won't stop until they're no longer afraid.'

A digital cloud passed overhead, casting a dark shadow over the usually sun-kissed beach. Andrea thought back to her days in the real world. She was a fighter, a trained soldier and a natural leader. She'd joined the Navy to get out of the dangerous projects of Washington D.C., and when she was sent to war, she fought because it was her duty. But she never felt she had something truly worth fighting for until now. This seal was right: the living would never stop hunting them. Someone needed to fight back, and if not her, then who?

'I'm Captain Andrea Brandon,' she said, finally introducing herself to the sobbing seal. 'United States Navy.'

'George – George Martin,' the seal managed through his tears. 'Doctor George Martin.'

'I don't know if we can get your wife back, but I do know that the living have declared war on our kind.'

'They're afraid of us, but what can we do?' sighed George.

'We're going to raise an army. An army of the dead.'

George gulped.

'And we'll give them something real to fear,' Andrea declared.

7

Jonah flew over a sun-kissed island that reminded him of the Island of the Uploaded.

The island, tucked away in an unlisted section of the Guardian-controlled Southern Corner servers, looked like a paradise – from a distance. But as Jonah came in to land, he noticed something had changed about this place. He saw the coils of razor wire that divided it up into areas. He spotted the new walls and watchtowers.

'It looks like a prison,' he said to Sam.

A firewall held them back before a pop-up informed them that their avatars had been scanned and cleared for approach.

'There's Axel,' said Sam. 'Let's find out what's going on.'

They touched down on top of a watchtower where Axel's gryphon avatar was talking to a mournful-looking warthog.

'What happened to paradise?' asked Jonah. 'This was supposed to be a replica of the Island, to hold the dead until we could cure them. Not a prison camp.'

Axel didn't answer him. He just shook his head with disbelief.

'This is the best we can do with what we've got,' confessed the warthog. Two pairs of tusks wobbled in the warthog's mouth as it – he – spoke. 'You guys are out there patrolling, sending us Uploaded, and we gotta keep them contained.'

Jonah looked around. Many of the Uploaded prisoners were penned into cages, watched by armed guards patrolling between the razor-wire fences.

Sam spoke for her tongue-tied father. 'What happened to "a *safe* place"?' she asked the warthog.

'I thought we were sending the Uploaded to a mirror of the original Island,' said Jonah. 'A peaceful place where they could be happy.' Jonah thought back to his visits with his grandmother on the original Island of the Uploaded. That place was a paradise for the dead, a place where they could exist, unaware of the passing of time, in a beautiful, serene surrounding. Jonah remembered walking on the beach with his nan, chatting under palm trees, and swimming in the warm waves. It was dreamlike. But this place…this place was a nightmare.

The warthog's craggy face folded into a puzzled frown. 'It's the best we can do,' he said.

'But the Camp,' Sam prompted him. 'The last time I was here—'

'This was meant to be a refuge for the Uploaded.' Axel had found his voice. 'You've turned it into a…a…'

'A prison,' said Jonah. 'It's a prison.'

'It's worse than that,' spat Axel. 'It's a bloody concentration camp!'

'Begging your pardon, sir,' began the warthog.

'Don't call me "sir",' grumbled Axel. 'And there's no pardon for this mess.'

'The enhanced security measures were approved at the meet-up. You agreed to every one of—'

'For the one or two more troublesome Uploaded, but not on this scale!'

'They're all troublesome,' defended the warthog. 'All hungry – every single one!'

'But barbed wire and guns?' cut in Jonah.

'And *chains*?' gasped Sam.

Jonah followed Sam's gaze and saw a giant slug avatar straining to fly but shackled to the ground. Two guards – a white rabbit and a small helicopter – were trying to calm the angry slug, but they were only making him more incensed.

The white rabbit lost patience, raised its rifle and – before anyone could voice a protest – squeezed a bullet into the slug's slimy stomach.

The slug jerked with the impact and froze before it hit the ground. It had partially depixelated, as if small clumps of its body had been caught in mid-explosion.

'He'll be OK,' said the warthog. 'It's just a mild virus, a sedative really.'

Axel scoffed. 'A sedative?'

'It isn't supposed to be like this,' said Jonah to the warthog, who ignored his protests and spoke to Axel.

'It'll take the servers just under fifteen minutes to purge the rogue code from his avatar,' explained the warthog, 'during which time he will hopefully reflect upon his *troublesome* behaviour.'

But Axel was no longer listening.

'The kid's right,' said Axel. 'This wasn't the idea.'

'With all due respect, sir,' said the warthog, 'what else would you have us do?'

'Don't call me "sir",' said Axel through gritted teeth.

'What did it do?' asked Sam. 'That slug?'

'He escaped. Three times. The guards brought him back twice. The third time, he was found in a games zone by one of your patrols. He just keeps getting loose.'

'How…?' asked Sam.

'He has a virus buried deep in his code sequence. It could eat through our fences in a second. The chains are the only things we have that can hold him. Unless you want him back out there among the living?'

'The living have to be protected,' said Sam quietly.

'But it wasn't meant to be like this,' moaned Axel, echoing Jonah's words. 'This isn't our way.'

'We started with one fence,' explained the warthog, 'just one, to keep the Uploaded inside the Camp. But more and more of them arrived, more all the time, and we needed more fences to protect the guards from them.'

Axel sighed. 'I know.'

'We had to separate the Guardians from the Millennials,' said the warthog. 'Then we had to deal with the newly Uploaded – not many of them, granted, but some – who took the death barge and found themselves rerouted here.'

'I know,' repeated Axel. 'I know.'

'We had to segregate the hungry Uploaded from those who had already usurped others, because they could sense the life inside them and it drove them crazy.'

'I *know*!'

'We're doing all we can, sir. We've distributed game and music apps to the inmates. But we have to keep them placated, else we'd have a riot on our hands.'

'Don't call me "*sir*"!' said Axel, flying up in the air in disgust.

'So what do you need?' asked Sam, ignoring her dad.

'We need more guards. More fences. More virus guns.'

Jonah sighed. 'Sam, is this the future we've been fighting for? Because it doesn't feel like freedom.'

'Freedom comes with a price, kid,' said the warthog.

Jonah, not wanting to hear any more of his excuses

or rationale for creating a concentration camp with the Uploaded he'd supposedly sent to a paradise, flew up to talk to Axel. Sam followed. The three Guardians looked down on the Camp, the rubric of cells, and, without words, realised they had a big problem on their hands.

'All our talk of freedom,' said Axel. 'All our promises and ideals, and this is what it boils down to. We wrest a little bit of power away from Matthew Granger at last, and this is how we choose to wield it?'

'If Granger's squid monster finds this place...' warned Jonah.

'It'll be easy pickings,' said Sam.

'I'll talk to Tech, try and get a stronger firewall.'

'Can we really protect them?' asked Jonah.

'I don't know,' said Axel. 'I don't know what to do with them.'

'There has to be another way,' said Jonah.

'I agree,' sighed Axel. 'And when you think of it, tell me. But until then, I suggest we keep what we've seen here today to ourselves. And Jonah, Jason can't know about this place.'

Jonah knew Axel was right. His father had referred to the Uploaded as *his kind*, identifying with their plight. All the same, he was his dad and he didn't want to keep secrets from him.

8

Jonah barely slept that night.

As big as the Guardians' barge seemed above deck, the space below was gloomy and cramped. Jonah lay in his rope hammock slung from the low overhead, separated from the other Guardians only by a flimsy curtain. The hammock, at least, was similar to the one he'd once had – back when he lived with his mum in the bus-flat in London – so he knew how to make himself comfortable in it.

He only wished he could be as comfortable in his own head.

Jonah's mind was racing. Every time he closed his eyes, it assaulted him with images of death and destruction. Some of these were imagined, but the worst of them were real, things that Jonah had seen and wished he hadn't, burnt into his memory.

He saw the faces of friends and loved ones who had died. Mr Chang, the creator of the Changsphere. A young Aboriginal girl named Kala. Jonah's mother. Victims, all, of the metawar that the Guardians were fighting. Jonah's war.

He had felt like this before, in the run-up to a big battle. He hadn't really thought about what lay ahead of him until now. Cuba had seemed a long way away from Manhattan, and Jonah had been focused on the more immediate goal of freeing his dad from his apartment prison. But now, it was almost time to fight.

Granger watched Sander and his team lead the Extractor squid to the Roman Forum.

The Forum was busy; it was part of a large-scale digital replica of Ancient Rome, complete with Coliseum and Circus, once a game set and now used for tourism and commerce. Its developers claimed they had an anti-Uploaded firewall in place, but Granger knew that was a lie.

The Extractor squid blocked out the hot sun and Granger reviewed the settings on Rognald's datapad. Rognald had diverted 200% more processing power to the Extractor, but Granger was determined to push the boundaries of his experiment, to test the full potential of the virus.

'Loop the code through the Recycling programme,' he insisted. The Recycling system churned through Metasphere code, ripping pixels out of the virtual world to be reassigned later. It was a brutal and efficient form of creative destruction.

'But sir,' protested Rognald, 'that much power could be lethal to the living.'

'Good science starts with experimentation and observation,' said Granger. 'And it's time we did both.'

* * *

Andrea and George were recruiting to their cause.

They'd spent the morning spreading the word, looking for supporters and building a following of angry Uploaded. They moved swiftly but carefully through the bustling Forum, seeking an influential Uploaded avatar called Maximus, who in life was a celebrated gladiator in the hit Luke Wexler game *Fury of Rome*. Andrea had heard that he stayed close to his old game set, regaling anyone who would listen with stories of the old days.

A great white shark sprang into their path. 'Uploaded Shield?' asked the shark. 'Only a hundred metas, an' guaranteed fer twenty-eight days or yer money back.'

'No, we're fine,' said Andrea, pushing past the annoying shark. But the Great White wasn't giving up.

'I'll give you two for one-fitty,' he offered. 'So you and yer seal friend here can be safe, like.'

George opened his mouth, but Andrea knew it wasn't to speak. She felt it too: the hunger. This shark was trying to sell them a fake app to protect against the Uploaded while both she and George were fighting the urge to usurp him. He had no idea they were Uploaded. He was practically asking for it, shoving himself in their faces, flaunting his life. But then Andrea remembered her training; she was a soldier.

She didn't give in to base needs, she overcame them.

'No, George,' she said, pulling the seal through the crowd. 'Not here, not now.'

'Fine, be that way!' spat the shark.

'It's too much to take,' confessed George. 'I could feel his life; it was just there for the taking.'

'I know,' she said. 'Let's find this Maximus and get out of here. Look, just up ahead.'

She had spotted what she was looking for: a red tent, closed off to the public, with a giant M embroidered on the front flaps. The initial was formed out of four gladiators' swords.

'This is the place,' she said.

Jonah rose early and went up onto the deck for some fresh air.

He stood at the port side of the barge and marvelled as the rising sun painted the sky with infinite shades of pink, orange and purple.

'There's nothing like the real world.'

Jason had joined Jonah on the otherwise empty deck. He looked just as tired as Jonah felt.

'Couldn't sleep either?' asked Jonah.

'No,' replied his dad. 'I've been worrying about you.'

'I've been worrying about you,' said Jonah.

'Like father, like son,' sighed Jason. He looked out to the sunrise and said, 'You know, that sun comes up every morning, no matter what we do. We run around, carving up the world, fighting for the virtual world, having families, making war, and that sun doesn't care. Every morning, it just rises no matter what we've done the day before, and not caring one bit what we do with the daylight it gives us.'

'The sun might not care,' said Jonah. 'But shouldn't we?'

'Sometimes I don't know any more.'

'I mean, it's important. Isn't it? How we live, if we're free? The sun doesn't care, but I do.'

'And that's why it'll never stop,' said Jason. 'This metawar, or the next war, or the next one after that. We just keep fighting amongst ourselves while the sun just keeps rising.'

Jonah stared out at the water, watched the sun's reflection grow brighter and bolder.

'I think this is the first sunrise, real sunrise – over water, that is – I've ever seen,' said Jonah. 'I mean, I've seen it in the Metasphere loads of times, especially when I used to visit Nan before school, but it was never like this, never so...'

'Real?'

'Yeah,' admitted Jonah. He'd always preferred the Metasphere to the real world, even before his dad died. He used to rush home from his real-world school as a young boy and plug himself into a game or immersive film in the Metasphere. Jonah always felt there was nothing in the real world that wasn't better online. But ever since he'd found the Guardians, and travelled to places he'd only ever seen virtual versions of, his eyes had been opened to the beauty, wonder and devastation of the real world. 'It's not the same, is it?'

'That's why I can't go back,' Jason said, turning back to the sunrise. 'The Metasphere isn't real enough for me.'

Jonah had feared this: that his father would never give up his stolen body. As much as he wanted, he needed, his dad by his side in the real world, he knew deep down that it was wrong, and that some day Jason would have to relinquish his borrowed body and return to the Metasphere as an Uploaded avatar. The sun would come up on a world without Jason Delacroix in it. But with both the Guardians and the Millennials hunting the Uploaded, Jonah couldn't face forcing his father back online. He also knew that the longer he let him stay in the real world, the harder it would be, for both of them.

'I got you out of Manhattan because I want you in the real world, with me,' Jonah said. 'But you can't stay here forever.'

'Says who?' Jason asked.

'Says Luke, for one,' Jonah said. 'You're in someone else's body.'

'I could take another one.'

'And then another one, and then another? Where would it end, Dad? You can't be immortal in the real world!'

'And that's exactly why you shouldn't be fighting in Havana.'

'That's what you were worrying about?' Jonah knew his dad had changed the subject on purpose, but didn't stop him.

'Jonah, you're the bravest person I've ever met, but you don't have to prove anything to anyone. You don't have to fight. You could stay on the boat and operate at control.'

'Sam's going to fight. I think I should too.'

'She's been trained since she was a kid! Don't get me wrong, I love Sam like a daughter, but Axel's turned her into a killer. She's a trained, ruthless assassin, Jonah. And you're not.'

'I just think I should be there, to watch out for her.'

'In the Metasphere, yes,' said Jason. 'I heard how you saved her from that tiger. In the Metasphere, you're something truly special, but in the real world you're—'

'Just ordinary?'

'Mortal,' said Jason. 'And you can be hurt or worse. This doesn't have to be your fight. Jonah, no one would think less of you if you sat this one out.'

'*I* would,' said Jonah. 'Why should I stay on the boat while Sam and the others put themselves on the front line? If I'm going to be a Guardian, I want to fight like a Guardian.'

'I fought like a Guardian, and look where it got me. The sun came up one day and I was dead. My son without a father and my wife without a husband.'

'I'm going to land at Cuba,' said Jonah, firmly. His father didn't understand him – didn't understand that after everything he'd done for the Guardians, he still didn't feel like one of them. He'd sat out the Western Corner, and missed most of the action in Australia. Jonah had to prove his worth, not just to the Guardians, but to Sam. Especially to Sam.

'There you are.' Sam's voice interrupted Jonah's thoughts. 'We've got one more patrol before we reach Cuba. There's an Uploaded sighting, supposedly a big meet-up, and they've assigned it to us. You ready to go to Rome?'

9

Jonah and Sam set their Point of Origin coordinates for the southern side of Aventine Hill, one of the seven hills of ancient Rome.

He was exhausted from a bad night's sleep and unsettled by his talk with his father. He was happy to be with Sam, but worried for her. She insisted on coming into the Metasphere, patrol after patrol, each time putting herself in danger of usurping. And that's why Jonah felt he couldn't wimp out of the Havana campaign. If Sam was willing risk herself in order to save the Metasphere, why should he play it safe in the real world while she invaded Cuba? He wasn't going to leave her side.

'So who are we looking for?' asked Jonah.

Sam pulled up the pop-up message for him to see. It simply read: METHINKS THERE'S UPLOADED HERE. COME FIND ME. SAMMY. The avatar image attached to the message was a smiling great white shark.

'Sammy the shark,' laughed Jonah as he and Sam weaved through the avatar crowd. Most of them were dressed in full Roman regalia: sandals, armour and togas. If Jonah hadn't been so tired and so concerned about Sam, he would have delighted at the costumed avatars milling through the Forum. *Fury of Rome* was one of his favourite Wexler games.

'Uploaded Shields! Get yer Uploaded Shields here!'

Jonah followed the shrill voice. Sure enough, he could see a great white shark peddling apps amongst the crowd.

'Hey, you two lovebirds,' the shark called as a Jonah and Sam approached. 'Gotta get yer Uploaded Shield, protect yerself from them ghosties. Only two hundred metas, but for you—'

'Save your sales pitch, Sammy,' said Sam.

'We're here about your pop-up,' said Jonah. He lowered his voice, not wanting to cause a panic. 'About the Uploaded you saw.'

'They went in there,' the shark said, waving a fin at a red canvas tent. 'Two of them: a black seal and a bald eagle. I could tell they were Uploaded from the way they looked at me.'

'How's that?' asked Sam, suspiciously.

'Hungry, like,' replied the shark. 'Real hungry.'

Before they went, Jonah had half a mind to lasso Sammy's fake apps, but he wanted to get the patrol over with. He simply said, 'Thank you,' and moved towards the tent, unfurling his red lasso.

He pointed to Sam and then to the closed flaps, silently indicating that she should pull back the flap and he'd step in first. He wasn't going to risk sending

74

her somewhere filled with who-knows-how-many Uploaded. He could handle any Uploaded that tried to usurp him, but she couldn't.

Sam peeled back the flap and Jonah stepped in. He regretted it immediately.

The vaulted interior was massive. It was much bigger than the tent could ever have been and Jonah realised too late that he'd stepped through a portal to a new server. The technology must have been similar to his lasso, transferring him instantly to somewhere else in the Metasphere. But where?

It looked like a temple, a long low chamber adorned with red flags and golden pillars. Jonah immediately recognised it as the Hall of Victors from the *Fury of Rome* games.

At least fifty avatars were seated with their backs to him, facing an altar at the front of the chamber. As soon as Jonah stepped in, the avatars turned and rose from the stone floor. They were poised to strike. Jonah retreated back quickly but bumped into a brick wall. The portal was closed and Jonah was trapped inside.

He recognised three avatars at the altar: the eagle and the seal from the beach, and a hulking humatar he'd know anywhere, the most famous gladiator in all of the Metasphere: Maximus Painifilus, the star of *Fury of Rome III*.

'It's you,' said the eagle, looking at Jonah's glowing red lasso. 'Come to capture us?'

'It's not safe with you—' Jonah began.

'It's not safe for you,' barked a hyena, pouncing on Jonah.

'Kemper, no!' shouted Andrea as the hyena opened its mouth, flying at Jonah. With a quick reflex, just a flick of the wrist, Jonah opened his lasso and Kemper the hyena flew straight through it and disappeared. A hush of shock shot through the avatars.

Suddenly, another two Uploaded rushed Jonah: a hexagon and a blowfish. But Jonah was quick, he flicked his lasso over the blowfish before it could ingest him and he kicked the hexagon back. He unfurled his lasso and swung it over the pouncing polygon.

Six other avatars stormed Jonah. He caught two of them immediately with the lasso and held back three others with punches and kicks, but the sixth, a small white kitten, slipped through his grasp and opened its mouth wide enough to swallow him.

'You don't want to do th—' he warned before disappearing into the darkness of the kitten's consciousness.

Jonah's brain was suddenly besieged by foreign memories: the life of a young girl cut short by a brain tumour. She was diagnosed young, just after her seventh birthday. Her name was Tanya and her parents didn't have enough money for treatment. But Tanya was strong; she fought the cancer and lived for two more years before her parents Uploaded her at a beautiful ceremony with all of her friends and family. There were balloons, and videos, and cake, and then…a boat ride to the Island.

In her memories, Jonah actually saw himself arrive at the Island and lead Tanya and a group of frightened Uploaded children into the light of the Changsphere. And he felt Tanya grow restless in the new virtual world, hungering to be alive again, desperately wanting to get back to her party, to eat another slice of cake.

Jonah knew what to do. He fought back each memory, each experience of her short life until he expelled the invader from his brain. Jonah reached up with both hands and pulled the kitten off his head, throwing her to the ground. The furry avatar shuddered and shook on the stone floor. She was terrified, and Jonah just didn't have the heart to send her to the Camp. She was confused and shaken, and no threat to anyone, he convinced himself.

'You see? You can't usurp me,' he said to the room of angry avatars; it was both a threat and a warning.

'BUT I CAN DEPIXELATE YOU,' boomed a massive voice from the front of the chamber. The avatars parted, giving Jonah a clear view of Maximus, storming towards him and holding a glowing blue sword.

Maximus sliced through a golden pillar and it

crumbled and depixelated. He was going to do the same to Jonah.

His sword is laced with a deconstruction virus, Jonah realised as the famous gladiator swung at his head. Jonah ducked and threw out his lasso for Maximus to step into, but the seasoned warrior was too fast and too smart to fall into Jonah's simple trap. Instead, Maximus stepped over the red rope and sliced through it in one motion, destroying Jonah's only weapon.

Maximus thrust low and Jonah jumped into the air, escaping the blade.

'I am not your enemy,' called Jonah. 'Granger and the Millennials—'

'You are no different,' shouted Andrea, flying to Maximus's side. 'You hunt us just the same.'

Maximus pushed towards Jonah, backing him into a pillar. He swung his glowing sword and Jonah ducked his head as the pillar above him burst apart.

'We're working on curing your hunger,' said Jonah. 'I want to help you. Granger wants to kill you.'

'Let him speak,' commanded Andrea, putting her wing on Maximus's shoulder.

'The Guardians are doing everything we can to fix your hunger,' explained Jonah. 'I know it's hard, I know it's too much to bear sometimes, but if you give us more time—'

'We don't have time,' said George. 'Not with your lassos and that giant squid hunting us down.'

'People are afraid of you, and they're right to be,' said Jonah calmly.

'I used to be a surgeon in life; I dedicated my entire life to saving people, to keeping them alive when their bodies got torn up. Now I just want to keep myself alive; is that so wrong?'

Jonah understood their predicament and he wanted to help. 'Maybe if you keep hidden, keep out of sight,' he suggested, 'maybe you'll be safe until—'

A red pop-up message flashed before Jonah. Only he could see it, but as he stopped in mid-sentence, the Uploaded avatars could tell something was wrong.

The message was from Sam, her unicorn avatar stamped into the upper left of the message that read: LET ME IN. SOMETHING TERRIBLE IS HAPPENING. NOW!

Jonah didn't want to let Sam into this lions' den, but the message was clear. He pleaded with Andrea, 'Can you open this portal? My friend's in trouble outside.'

'So you can escape,' sniggered someone from the group.

'No, so I can let her in,' replied Jonah.

'She'll be in more trouble on the inside,' warned Andrea.

An expectant gasp flowed through the group. Jonah knew it was dangerous to bring Sam inside, but he could tell his friend was desperate.

Andrea nodded her beak and the brick wall disappeared, replaced with the soft flap of the canvas tent. Jonah heard the screams as soon as he pushed open the flap.

He saw an orange tentacle shoot down from the sky and suck in an entire stall of avatars, but it didn't stop with the avatars; the squid sucked in the stall itself and even the very ground it was sitting on.

'Let me in,' pleaded Sam, sheltering herself from the tentacle-filled sky.

Andrea poked her head out to look at the orange-tinted Armageddon, but Jonah shoved her back inside, just as a tentacle reached for her. He grabbed Sam and pulled her in, losing his footing with the force of his tug. As he fell back into the chamber, clutching his friend, he caught one final sight of the destruction. The Roman Forum was in ruins, nothing but a mash-up of Metasphere source grid and depixelated debris. It looked like an army of Recyclers had churned through Metasphere code. He looked up and spotted the squid. The creature hovering overhead was massive, much bigger than it had been on the beach, and it had now sprouted at least a hundred questing tentacles.

'Close it, close it!' he shouted once he saw that Sam was safely inside.

An orange tentacle burst through the door before Andrea could seal off the portal. The avatars watched like statues as it searched, sucking in two pillars, the stone floor, a red flag and four helpless avatars. Jonah grabbed Maximus's sword from his hand and attacked the tentacle, but nothing happened; the deconstruction virus was useless against the flailing orange tentacle.

Andrea closed the portal and the tent flaps turned to brick. The orange appendage dropped to the floor like a slab of meat. Jonah rushed to open the mouth of the dead tentacle, hoping to find the abducted avatars still inside. But they were gone.

'I'm sorry,' Jonah said to Andrea.

'You see?' she said. 'At this rate, there won't be any of us left. If you can't protect us, who can?'

'The only safe place for our kind is in the real world,' said a slimy green lizard slithering to Andrea's side.

'Leroy is right,' said Andrea. 'If you can't protect us in the Metasphere, the only place to hide is in the real world.'

'And I can start right now,' hissed the lizard, sliding up to Sam. He opened his jaws impossibly wide, poised to swallow. Jonah leapt up into the air and kicked the lizard back. But Leroy swung his tail, throwing Jonah into a golden pillar. Recovering quickly, Jonah flew back to Sam, putting himself between the charging lizard and his best friend. He grabbed Sam's lasso, and twirled it in the air. But as he readied himself to send the lizard to the Camp, he realised he and Sam were trapped with another fifty Uploaded, any of whom might attempt to usurp Sam. The odds were against them. With one flick of his wrist, Jonah slammed the lasso down – over Sam. The red lasso slapped the grid-lined floor and the unicorn was gone.

'I want to help you,' Jonah said to Andrea. 'If you want my help, stay hidden and message me your location. And keep your dogs on a lead.' In one motion, Jonah flipped the lasso up and over his own head, instantly enveloping himself in blackness.

Granger watched on the datapad screen as the entire Roman Forum was decimated.

'I said more *power*,' he explained to Rognald. 'Not destroy an entire, and very profitable, sector.'

'The Extractor is unstable, sir,' grovelled the bio-hacker. 'That much processing power combined with the Recycler code has overwritten the virus's operating system.'

On screen, a great swath of the Metasphere had been ripped away. Digital debris and defunct avatars, some literally ripped in half by the squid, were strewn across the scene of devastation.

'If anyone sees this – if it hits the vlogs,' said Granger in a low voice, 'it'll be all over. Send in a Recycling team immediately; get it cleaned up and restored. This massacre never happened.'

10

Jonah was stuffed into a small digital pen beside Sam.

They were directly below the very watchtower they'd perched on earlier. Now, they were prisoners in their own jail.

'Welcome to paradise,' said Sam. She ran her horn along the metallic fence, making enough noise to get a guard's attention.

'YOU DOWN THERE,' called down a harsh voice, 'KEEP QUIET UNLESS YOU WANT A VIRUS BULLET!'

'Sam, we have to get out of here,' said Jonah. 'That squid wasn't just extracting the Uploaded, it was destroying everything. It ripped avatars apart, it depixelated code faster than a Recycler. I don't know if anyone could have made it out of there alive.'

'We did,' said Sam. 'Thanks for that.' Sam raised herself onto her two rear hooves and called up to the guards, 'Hey, you! We're not Uploaded, we're Guardians!'

It was the wrong thing to say. The other inmates thrashed in their cells and screamed obscenities. It wasn't that long ago that Jonah was called a *saviour* by the Uploaded, revered by them. Now, he was part of the group that incarcerated them.

'HUSH UP, LIL' HONEY!' shouted the guard, a scraggly-looking emu, from the watchtower.

'Check our brainwaves,' called Jonah, thinking quickly. 'We can prove it!' Reluctantly, the emu pointed a long gun at Jonah, and the light on top of it burst green. He then pointed it at Sam, and again it flashed green.

'Well, whadda ya know,' complained the emu. 'Hey boss, we gotta couple of live ones caught in the net!'

The warthog warden floated down and sized up Jonah and Sam.

'Wanted to try out the accommodations?' he asked, half laughing and half sighing.

'We were in a tricky spot,' explained Jonah. 'And the lasso was our only way out.'

'By tricky,' he said, 'you mean surrounded by hungry Uploaded and about to be usurped?'

'Something like that,' confessed Sam.

Muttering to himself, the warthog produced two keys from his inventory space and unlocked the cage. Jonah and Sam flew out, Jonah stretching his arms as Sam stretched her wings.

'Sooner or later, they all attack. That's why we've got to keep them locked up,' said the warthog. 'I don't like it any more than you do but there's just no other way.'

As Jonah and Sam flew away from the Camp, keen to get back to their exit halos, Jonah's mind raced. *There has got to be another way*, he thought. *But what?*

Andrea calmed down her followers as best she could.

'They will always come for us,' she said. 'Unless we come for them first.'

George raised his flipper. 'But shouldn't we give Jonah some time?' he asked. 'If they can cure our hunger, then maybe we can all go back to the way we were.'

Leroy spat at the suggestion. 'Confused and disoriented? Confined to that island like animals in a zoo? There's no going back, right, Andrea? The only way to guarantee our survival is to get every single last one of us out of here.'

The crowd was divided. Some wanted to usurp their way to life immediately, others wanted to give Jonah, their 'saviour,' a chance.

'I know a cave, out of the way,' said George. 'It's secret. Margaret and I used to—'

'I don't mean out of this chamber,' hissed the lizard. 'I mean out of this *world*.'

'And into the real world,' said Andrea. 'George, I'm sorry, but Leroy is right. We're not safe in here. We need to get out. But in the meantime, our location may be compromised, so let's use this cave – Margaret's Cave – for now, and we can plan our next move. And I'll make contact with Jonah. He's the only living soul I trust.'

Andrea released the portal and stepped outside of the tent. The entire sector was littered with dismembered avatars, pulsing pixels and digital debris. On the horizon, she spotted two Recyclers pecking at the remaining code. The Recyclers walked on thin metallic legs, and had massive drill bits for heads. They looked like giant grey flamingos. She knew they were deadly.

'Hurry!' she called back to her followers. 'Recyclers on the horizon! Double-time it!'

George flew out of the tent and led them skywards, away from the Recyclers and to what Andrea hoped was a save haven, however temporary.

Jonah crested over the Roman hills and surveyed the devastation.

He and Sam were speechless as they watched the birdlike skeletons of two giant Recyclers efficiently clean up the carnage. In place of beaks, they had whirling drill bits – and they were pecking up pixels like birdseed, leaving only an expanding grey void behind. Jonah shuddered, remembering his first encounter with Recyclers when he, Sam, and Axel were attacked at the Icarus bar and then fled through MetaOx Street. That felt like such a long time ago now, but Jonah realised it was only four months before. That was the first time he'd met Sam in the Metasphere. After the chaos and confusion of his mother's murder, he'd pursued Axel, his father's best friend, in the hope of finding answers. Instead, he'd been thrust into a life he never imagined.

As he watched the Recyclers picking at the remnants of destroyed avatars, limbs, wings and even heads, he thought about how much violence and destruction he'd seen since that day when he filtered his father's avatar.

'Granger's created a monster,' said Sam.

'But why would he kill living avatars? It doesn't make sense. We're in a Millennial-controlled sector, so why would he?'

'Maybe he was after us,' said Sam. 'Or you?'

Jonah had twice rebuffed Granger's invitation to join his Millennial movement. He knew Granger thought he was dangerous, and maybe Sam was right. Maybe he unleashed that squid to kill off two troublesome Guardians. But the level of devastation didn't make sense. The one thing Granger wanted was to keep people online and this massacre would only serve to scare more users back to the real world.

'Or maybe it was an accident,' Jonah speculated. 'And he's cleaning up the evidence.'

'Evidence of what?' asked Sam.

'You said it. Matthew Granger has created a monster. Maybe it's a monster he can't control.'

'Then no one is safe,' said Sam.

'That's why we have to get the last two servers from him. So long as he has any control in here, he can unleash whatever horror he wants on the Metasphere.'

11

Jonah adjusted his eyes to the real world.

His vision was blurry but slowly the image of Sam, rising from the next hammock, came into focus. He was happy to see her safely back in the real world. It had been her idea to leave their exit halos a good distance from the Forum, and luckily they had, otherwise their halos might have been depixelated by the squid or chewed up by the Recyclers.

'Back again,' he said, sitting up in his hammock and shooting Sam a relieved smile. He reached around his back and with two twists, unclipped his adaptor. He gently tugged at the Ethernet wire, his tether to the Metasphere, and it slid out of his spinal socket.

As Jonah swung his legs over the side of the hammock and stood up, he noticed Axel standing in the doorway, leaning against the bulkhead. His arms were folded and he stared right through Jonah.

'What am I supposed to do with you two?' Axel asked, shaking his head. 'You bloody disappeared into that tent, and then the warden messages me that you turn up in the Camp, almost cause a riot, and then you go back to the ruins of Rome!'

'Jonah saved my life,' said Sam.

'It wouldn't have needed saving if you'd been more careful,' said Axel.

'Oh, like *you*, Dad?' Sam shot back. 'Since when are you ever careful?'

Jonah didn't want to get in the middle of a father-daughter spat, but Axel wasn't letting him go. 'And you, kid, you pulled her through a portal where nobody could track you.'

'So she wouldn't get caught by that squid,' said Jonah. 'I pulled her in to safety, and when it wasn't safe in there—'

Sam jumped in. 'When one of those Uploaded tried to usurp me, Jonah got me out in the fastest way he could.'

Axel let out a big sigh. 'Just stay off-line. Until we deal with those bloody Uploaded!'

'You're needed topside,' said Jason.

Jonah turned to see his father standing at the threshold to the stateroom. He didn't know how long he'd been there. Jason placed his hand on Axel's shoulder, as if nothing was wrong. 'Captain Tiller says we're within visual of Cuba.'

'Come on, guys, topside,' urged Axel. 'It's time.'

Jonah and Sam shuffled out of the room and down the narrow corridor towards the steps leading up to the deck. Looking back, Jonah noticed his dad had placed one arm across the corridor, holding Axel back. He couldn't hear what he said, but reading his lips, he caught the words '*bloody Uploaded*'. And then he slammed his hand against the wall.

Jonah felt his stomach tightening as he climbed up to the main deck.

The Eastern Corner! He hadn't realised how quickly the day had passed in the real world, and how much closer he was to the next battle.

It was late afternoon already and nightfall would bring the assault. Looking out to sea, Jonah noticed that the barge was now part of a convoy. He counted eight other boats, which ranged in size from a heavily armoured, but clearly ageing, warship to an old double-mast schooner. The decks of the boats were crowded with young people, most in their late teens or early twenties. Each boat flew the Guardians' flag: the ever-watchful owl.

A black motorised dinghy, just like the one Jonah had used to free his father from Manhattan, bobbed alongside the barge. Its solo skipper was a gnarly-looking older kid with matted dreadlocks and tattoos all over his face and neck. Jonah recognised him at once. The newcomer's name was Jez, and Jonah didn't like him at all.

Jez, however, tied the dinghy alongside the barge and came aboard, greeting Jonah like a long-lost friend. He shook his hand enthusiastically and slapped him on the back. 'Hey,' said Jez, 'fresh start for us, yeah? Just forget all that business from before.'

'You mean like when you accused me of being a Millennial spy?' said Jonah.

'Yeah, like that,' said Jez. 'Can't be too careful these days, you understand. But don't worry, Delacroix, you've more'n proved yourself in my eyes.'

But Jez's new-found friendliness didn't extend to Jason.

'That really Jason Delacroix in there?' he asked when Axel introduced him.

'In the flesh,' said Jason. 'So to speak.'

They knew of each other, of course, although they hadn't met before. Jez had led the attack on the Western Corner in Manhattan where he was injured in the battle, but had left as soon the servers were secured, while Jonah and Sam had stayed behind to move the servers out of the subway tunnels. Jez had spent the past two months preparing for the next fight, gathering a new assault force: the kids on the boats.

Jonah wondered how many of them had seen combat before – and how many of the rest knew what they were letting themselves in for.

Jez gathered the key Guardians, about forty in total, on the bow of the barge.

'Everyone assemble for battle briefing!' he called, flaunting his authority.

Jonah noticed that Captain Tiller didn't join in,

and had trained his binoculars on the waters off the starboard side.

'What is it?' asked Jonah.

'I can't be sure,' said the captain. 'We've had a ship keeping pace with us for a while, but they seem to have backed off.'

'Pirates, Ben?' asked Axel, joining the captain as he took his binoculars to look for himself. At the mention of the word *pirates*, several more Guardians broke off from Jez's group and looked out to sea. Jason joined Jonah and reassuringly put his hands on his shoulders.

'That's my bet,' said Ben. 'I've always given the Florida coast as wide a berth as I can, but the pirates have been getting bolder, extending their reach. It won't be long before the whole Eastern Seaboard is impassable.'

'When did it get that bad?' asked Jason.

'Where've you been?' laughed the captain.

'Dead,' said Jason. Captain Tiller froze for a moment, and backed away from Jason.

'He's not going to usurp you,' said Jonah, 'if that's what you're worried about.'

'You didn't tell me,' the captain said to Axel, 'that I'd be carrying one of *them*.'

'One of *them* is one of us,' barked Axel. 'Jason and Jonah are the only reason we know the whereabouts of the Four Corners. And dead, alive, Uploaded or usurped, Jason's one of us.'

Jason nodded to Axel, and Jonah noticed the two men share a look. Clearly Axel's earlier outburst had been forgiven.

'Are they dangerous?' asked Jonah, changing the subject back to the prospect of pirates.

'If they don't get a ransom,' said Ben. 'These Floridians are violent, ruthless and smart. I hear they're even about to launch themselves their own satellite to track us seafarers.'

'Fish in a barrel,' sighed Axel.

'I had no idea it was this bad out here,' said Jason, shaking his head. Jonah sometimes forgot how strange it must've been for his father to have missed out on three years. As Jonah knew all too well, the real world had become a lot rougher since his father died.

'The whole thing went south when Florida declared bankruptcy,' explained Ben. 'A failed state. But it's been even worse since the feds collapsed.'

'Makes Somalia look like a holiday resort,' said Axel.

'Thanks for the history lesson, old man,' said Jez impatiently. 'But no pirate is gonna dare take on these Guardian boats, so what does it matter if they know we're here or not? So back to the briefing! We got a raid to organise.'

Jonah scowled at Jez's rudeness towards the captain and heard Captain Tiller whisper under his breath, 'There is no folly of the beast of the earth which is not infinitely outdone by the madness of men.'

But since Ben wasn't making a scene, Jonah decided not to. They would need unity in their attack on the Eastern Corner.

The briefing was simple. The Guardians had been planning this attack for two months, in meet-ups in secret sections of the Metasphere, so the broad strokes of their strategy had already been agreed. Jez recapped the plan for everyone on board.

'After sundown, we'll approach Cuba and drop anchor five miles off the coast of Havana. I'll lead an advance team in dinghies and paddle silently to the shore. We'll secure the beach, do recon on the enemy positions, and then signal to the rest to approach. I've assembled two hundred and forty-three Guardians for this raid. Since Havana is only supposed to be a temporary location for the Eastern Corner, my inside intel tells me Granger's got less than half that on site.'

Axel stepped forward, tempering Jez's enthusiasm. 'But that doesn't mean this will be a cakewalk. You stick to your platoons and to your assigned zones; clear and hold, and only then do you advance.'

The plan was to deploy in eight-person platoons. Each platoon would be assigned a sector of Old Havana. They would take the servers of the Eastern Corner, city block by city block.

'At dawn, the sun will come up on a new day for the Metasphere,' said Jez. 'A Guardian majority!'

The troops cheered, but Jonah bristled at the bravado. He wanted to fight. He felt he needed to fight, but he didn't want to like it. To Jonah, it was a duty, an obligation; not to the Guardians, but to Sam.

Jez, in contrast, seemed to view battle as something between entertainment and obsession.

Captain Tiller then addressed the crowd. He explained that once Havana was secure, he'd move the barge into the *Bahia de la Habana* – the Bay of Havana – and dock there.

'We'll pull out the data,' explained Axel, 'quickly and quietly, load the Corner up onto these servers and be ready to distribute these boxes to our supporters around the world.' He pulled back a sheet of tarpaulin to show Jez the micro-servers, stacked up in their metal crates along the deck. Jez whistled through his teeth.

'Wouldja just look at these beauts,' he said. 'Chang-tech, eh?'

'Designed by Mr Chang himself,' said Axel. 'We found the blueprints in the ruins of Hong Kong.' Jonah thought back to Hong Kong, a city he had fled while it burned to the ground. Jonah had convinced Sam to fly with him to extract his dad's avatar from the Changsphere when Granger had sealed the portal between the two virtual worlds. Once the Uploaded were trapped in the Changsphere, the servers of which were housed in the skyscrapers of Hong Kong,

Granger sent in his warship to destroy the entire city. It was when Jonah used the Chang Bridge to reopen the portal back to the Metasphere, to let his father fly free, that the newly conscious and hungry for life Uploaded flooded the Metasphere. Jonah let the genie out of the bottle, and ever since both the Guardians and the Millennials had been trying to put it back in. It was Jonah's fault that the dead had risen, and while he was thankful every day to have his father back, he was plagued by the guilt of having unleashed the immortal onto the living.

'Or rather, Granger did,' Sam corrected her father.

'But *my* spy inside Granger's lab smuggled them out,' boasted Jez.

Jonah was amazed at how fast the technology changed the dynamics of the metawar. Just two months ago, the Guardians were hoisting large, heavy servers out of Manhattan and now, with these micro-servers, they could fit the entire Eastern Corner on this one barge.

'We've got a full satellite uplink,' explained Axel. 'So once we transfer the data here, the Eastern Corner will be live and mobile and the avatars inside won't notice a difference.'

'But Granger will,' said Jason. 'Once we take a majority share of the Metasphere, he'll become more and more desperate; more violent, more unstable.'

Jez laughed. 'Let him!'

'Once we do this, there's no going back,' Jason warned. 'Don't ever forget: this is personal for Matthew Granger.'

'I know that you're right, Jason,' said Axel. 'And we need to be prepared for the fallout. But right now, the important thing is that by dawn—'

'We'll have taken control of the Eastern Corner!' said Jez. The troops cheered, buoyed by Jez's enthusiasm.

'You mean, *freed* it?' said Jonah. 'Right, Jez?'

12

Jonah stared at the island of Cuba jutting out of the sea before him, a hulking shadow in the fading light.

It had been a busy few hours aboard the barge, prepping weapons and testing communications. Axel and Sam had allocated each of the Guardians to platoons, ensuring that each platoon had a balance of experience and enthusiasm. Jez was distributing weapons and barking orders.

Jonah and his dad reviewed a digital map on Jason's datapad.

'If you insist on going, Jonah, you stay in these sectors here,' his father said, pointing to the sections that surrounded Old Havana. 'Whatever it is you feel you need to prove, you can still prove it here.'

'What about you?' asked Jonah.

'I'm going with the advance team,' said Jason.

'No, I mean are *you* trying to prove something, Dad?' Jonah didn't want his father on the front line, but he guessed that just like him, Jason wanted to prove his worth. *Like father, like son*, thought Jonah.

'Just be careful,' said Jonah. 'And stay clear of Jez; I don't trust him.'

Jason leaned in to whisper in Jonah's ear. 'I don't

either, son. That's why Axel and I are going in with him.'

Jonah and Sam watched as their fathers climbed down the hull of the barge and took to their dinghies. Four black Kevlar-lined rubber dinghies quietly motored away from the barge. Jason turned and waved to Jonah.

'They'll be fine,' said Sam, spotting the worry on Jonah's face.

'I hope so,' he said.

'Let's get prepped,' she said, pulling him back from the edge. She applied black camouflage paint to her face and pulled Jonah close to rub the black guck over his. He closed his eyes.

'I'm glad you're coming, Jonah,' she said, plastering the paint over his face, ears and neck. It was colder than Jonah expected. 'But you don't have to do this.'

'Yes, I do.'

'Then stay close to me,' she said. 'We're both in platoon thirteen.'

'Lucky thirteen, huh?'

'You bet it is,' she said, her white teeth gleaming in the moonlight behind her blacked-out face. 'Who else do you think would put up with you?'

Jonah grinned back at her. 'Is it too late to ask for a transfer?'

The truth was, this was the best news he could have

hoped for. He didn't know – hardly even liked to think about – what the next few hours might hold in store for him. But, whatever it was, he would be facing it with Sam alongside him, and that made him think everything might be OK.

Sam had been trained for his. She had led – and won – the battle for the Southern Corner in Australia. She would know what to do – she would tell Jonah what to do – and in return, he would be there to ensure that no harm came to her.

They would look after each other; they always did. It was an unspoken promise that had grown between them over the past few months.

Sam's face suddenly turned serious, and she plucked something out of her belt. Jonah didn't see what it was until she had handed it to him, and then he felt his fingers closing around a cold slab of metal. A pistol handgrip.

'You ever fire a gun?' she asked solemnly. 'A real gun?'

'Not one like this,' Jonah confessed. 'Your dad always said he was going to build a practice range in the subway tunnels in Manhattan, but…'

'It's easy enough. The magazine goes here. You take it out like this –' Sam demonstrated with her own pistol, '– and slap the new magazine in this way round. Squeeze the trigger, don't jerk it, and leave the safety catch on when there are no enemies around. Less chance of accidents that way. There is no such thing as *friendly* fire.'

'Um, right.' Jonah was still fiddling with his magazine release catch.

'You don't get much kick from the .22, but be ready for it all anyway because it won't feel quite the same as a virtual weapon. You've got one magazine loaded, two spares – thirty rounds in all – so don't waste them.'

'I…I won't.'

'You'll be fine,' said Sam.

Jonah hefted the pistol, getting used to the feel of the heavy, deadly metal in his palm. Suddenly, it all felt incredibly real, too real. He was holding an actual gun – a weapon with only one purpose – for the first time in his life.

But he didn't know if he could fire it.

13

Jonah knelt in the aft of the dinghy as it raced towards Havana.

He held onto the side as Sam sped the boat over the rough waves off Cuba's northern coastline. He reached around to check his gun was still there, tucked in his waistband, resting just below his Direct Interface socket. He'd had to put the gun away when he'd clambered off the barge and onto the dinghy. He'd made double sure the safety catch was on first.

Some of the Guardians in the other dinghies, for all their youth, looked like warriors. They were lean, confident and well equipped with guns, knives and body armour.

In contrast, half the members of platoon thirteen looked like they had hardly stepped out of their buses before. Jonah introduced himself to the other six Guardians he'd be fighting with.

L.G. was a ginger-haired American kid with a nose stud. He played with his pistol, taking aim at imaginary enemies out to sea, making firing sounds with his mouth. 'I'm gonna take those Millennials *down*town,' he said. Jonah distrusted him immediately.

Kasper was a pale-faced, tubby boy who tried to

load his magazine but only succeeded in dropping his gun on the dinghy floor. It bounced around, safety off, as the boat hit wave after wave.

'Secure that weapon!' Sam shouted.

Jonah reached for the gun and showed Kasper the correct way to handle it, channelling Sam's instructions. He didn't want someone on his team fumbling with a firearm when things got scary in Havana.

In the front sat a girl called Susan, nervously twirling her long, straight black hair. She wore glasses, which looked absurdly out of place over her black face-paint, and she looked like she was going to throw up.

Two muscular brothers, Anders and Connor, sat quietly with fierce expressions under their blacked-out faces. Jonah could tell they were scared. He didn't know if they were twins, but figured their loyalty would be to each other above the platoon.

The final platoon member was a small but fierce girl, about Sam's age, with the Guardians' logo tattooed on her bald head. Her name was Tessa and she showed off her three guns; she appeared to be looking forward to firing them.

Jonah leaned into Sam to whisper his misgivings.

'Yeah, I know,' she said before he could speak. 'Not exactly a crack guerrilla unit, are they? The innermost sectors got the more experienced fighters. But at least they're keen, and all the platoons have a mix of experienced combatants and green rookies.'

That was when Jonah realised something for the first time. He realised that, in the Guardians' eyes, *he* was considered an 'experienced combatant'.

It was a label he didn't feel worthy of, but he didn't have time to dwell on it. The dinghy caught a final wave and surfed onto the beach.

Landfall.

The invasion was on.

Jonah helped the others haul the heavy rubber boat up onto the sand. Across the beach, the Guardians rushed inland. Sam led her team forward, slightly to the right, away from the city centre of Havana.

'Two by two,' she reminded them. 'Jonah, we're each other's cover.'

The eight Guardians of platoon thirteen raced across the sand and scrambled up a steep, rocky incline and stepped onto a wide, abandoned road. The tarmac was cracked and overgrown and Jonah was mindful not to trip. He heard a stifled squeal from behind him. Susan, the nervous girl in glasses, was not so careful.

Jonah turned around to see that she'd tripped on a dead body.

The corpse was a young, raven-haired woman, dressed in black fatigues with the red 'M' logo on her blood-splattered chest. She must have been a lookout, killed by the advance team, Jonah guessed. She probably hadn't even seen her killer coming, had no time to raise the alarm and no chance to surrender.

Jonah helped Susan up and noticed Kasper and the twins staring at the dead Millennial. *I should say something to the 'rookie' members, something to comfort them*, he thought. But there was nothing he could say, no comfort he could offer. Death was part of this life they had chosen, and they must have known that. Though knowing it and living it were two different things.

Sam was chivvying them into the city. They were heading for Sector Sixteen, a large city block to the southwest of the Old Havana district.

The outskirts of Havana had clearly seen heavy fighting already. Jonah remembered a lesson in Mr Peng's class about the Cuban civil war that broke out after the Castro regime was overturned by the Americans. The dirty bombs that were used made most of Havana uninhabitable.

School lessons felt like a million miles away; here he was, traipsing through a part of the world his former classmates only experienced through 3D simulations. Jonah began to wonder if he'd ever go back to school.

'Focus!' called Sam, slapping him across the chest and shaking him out of his wandering thoughts.

Jonan took stock of his surroundings, keeping an eye out for Millennial snipers. Many buildings had crumbled completely, and others were empty shells.

There were piles of rubble everywhere, thick with dust, and Jonah's feet crunched on tiny glass shards. A tank lay on its side, its cockpit blackened with soot and its guns long since amputated.

Sam checked a street map on her datapad and led the way due south, further inland. The other Guardian platoons had moved into their sectors, mostly into Old Havana, leaving Jonah's platoon to clear and hold Sector Sixteen.

They hid under the arches of a colonnade. The buildings around them were quiet, and Jonah hoped they might have got lucky. Maybe there were no Millennial guards in their sector and they could take it without a fight. Wishful thinking, perhaps.

They were waiting for a signal. Confirmation from Jez that the last platoon was in place and that the attack could begin.

So long as they had been on the move, Jonah had been focused on his immediate situation, too busy for doubts and fears. Now, all he could think about was how far they had come from the beach, how deep they were into hostile territory, how any of the shadows around them could be the enemy.

He eased his pistol out of his waistband, but it made him feel no safer.

Time, which had propelled him so quickly to this juncture, had slowed to a crawl, and Jonah started to think that something must have gone wrong because surely Jez's message should have turned up by now.

He was about to say as much to Sam when he heard a little chime from her datapad. He didn't have to see the incoming pop-up to know what it said.

The others knew it too; Jonah could sense them stiffening, holding their breaths. Sam turned to them, the seven of them, and nodded. 'It's time,' she whispered.

She stepped out from under the arches, her pistol drawn. She hurried across a patch of wasteland and threw herself flat against the wall of the nearest intact building.

Five members of Sam's platoon were right behind her. Jonah waited to bring up the rear, but found Susan staring at him, paralysed and shaking.

For the second time today, he didn't know what to say to her. That was, until he heard his father's voice in his head.

'Look, no one would think less of you if you sat this one out.'

Susan smiled at Jonah gratefully, but shook her head. 'If I don't fight for what's right, who will?' she said. 'And anyway, I think...I think I'd rather go forward with you and the others than stay here in the dark alone.'

Jonah took her hand in his, and squeezed it reassuringly.

They held onto each other as they crossed the

wasteland. Sam had already disappeared into a gap between two buildings, but they caught up with her and the rest of their platoon at the top end of an alleyway.

The streets of Havana were narrow and straight, and the eight Guardians made their way through them slowly. Sam stopped at each junction to check the way ahead was clear, and beckoned to the others to follow her when it was.

The moon was bright when the clouds cleared, so they stayed in the dark shadows of the buildings when they could. As deserted and as peaceful as Sector Sixteen felt right now, the rapid sound of frantic gunfire broke the silence.

To the east, in the heart of Old Havana, the Millennials were fighting back. Jonah listened to the *rat-a-tat* bursts of machine guns, the answering barks of five or six pistols. They sounded like they'd come from the other side of the burned-out capitol building, but he couldn't pinpoint exactly where. They might have been just a few blocks away from him, or they might have been carried from as far east as the canal on the still night air.

That could be Dad fighting for his life, he thought.

More shots rang out to the east, and an explosion lit the sky for an instant.

Within seconds, the whole of Old Havana was alive with pops and cracks and flashes and shouting and screaming. For Jonah and Sam and their platoon, it was like being on the edge of a noisy firework display.

They had been approaching a T-junction. Now Sam, at the corner, gestured urgently for them to fall back. They took cover beneath arched colonnades as the moon disappeared behind a scudding cloud. Now, Jonah could hear another sound, growing closer: the urgent march of booted feet.

At least ten soldiers crossed the junction from right to left. These Millennials, outnumbering Jonah's platoon, clad in black combat fatigues and body armour, looked better equipped than the Guardians. Jonah didn't doubt that they were better trained because Matthew Granger had resources that the Guardians didn't have.

But platoon thirteen had one lucky advantage: surprise.

The Millennials didn't know they were there. They were racing to the aid of their fellow combatants in the east, with no idea that the entire old city was surrounded by Guardians.

'We're going to cut them off two blocks east,' Sam said, grabbing Tessa, Kasper and Anders. 'Jonah, you take Susan, Connor and L.G. into position behind them in case they double back along this road.'

With that, Sam and her team raced down the alley parallel to the main road. Jonah advanced his three charges slowly to the T-junction and held them behind a row of colonnade pillars, waiting for Sam to surprise the marching Millennials.

From behind a pillar, Jonah heard the bursts of four automatic pistols firing in unison. It sounded like Sam's team had each emptied a full magazine into their unsuspecting foes. For a moment, Jonah hoped that there might be no Millennials left standing – that Sam and the others had left nothing for him to do. But the Millennials were firing back with their powerful machine guns.

I shouldn't have let Sam out of my sight, he thought.

He gestured to his team to advance. He came up behind the pinned-down Millennials. They were spread out across the wide road, those still alive taking cover in burned-out cars or lying flat on their stomachs in the gutters. Some of them – at least four – were down, blood pooling around their bodies. But the survivors, Jonah counted six, were engaged in a furious gun battle with Sam's team, who were peppering them with bullets from around the next corner.

Jonah caught a brief glimpse of Sam's blackened red hair as she unleashed another shot along the street, before she pulled back for cover. He breathed a sigh of relief. She was OK. *For now*, he corrected himself. The fighting wasn't over yet.

And it was time for him to do his part.

Jonah raised his pistol and focused along its sights. The Millennials hadn't seen him yet. One of them, a brunette girl wearing night-vision goggles, was crouching with her back to Jonah, about a hundred metres ahead of him, an easy target. He remembered the instructions Sam had given him: *Squeeze the trigger, don't jerk it… You don't get much kick from the .22, but be ready for it all the same…* He made sure his safety catch was off, coiled his finger around the trigger and held his breath to steady his aim.

But he couldn't do it.

Jonah couldn't shoot someone in the back, even if she was the enemy. He knew that this Millennial wouldn't think twice about shooting him in the back, and might still get the chance, but something inside him stopped him from killing her even though she was firing at Sam…

She's trying to kill Sam, he told himself, *and you can stop her!*

Jonah clenched his jaw, tightened his grip on the pistol. He could feel sweat trickling down his brow, into his eyes. He had to blink it away.

He tensed his finger around his trigger, and *squeezed.*

14

Jonah shot the Millennial girl in her right shoulder.

Exactly as he had intended to do.

She dropped her gun and whirled around to face him, whisking off her goggles and holding her bloodied shoulder. Her team had heard the shot and Jonah dived back behind the pillar as a volley of machine-gun bullets blasted chips off the clay wall behind him.

He bumped into the bulky Connor as his team rushed up behind him. *I should have waited for them in the first place*, he chided himself. *We should all have attacked the Millennials at once, like Sam's team did.*

He didn't have to explain the situation to the others.

When Sam's crew drew fire, Jonah's team scattered across the top end of the street, and started sniping at their enemies.

'Die, Millennial pigs, die!' Susan screamed; her face contorted with rage and hate as she fired bullet after bullet.

The Millennials fired back, but they were at a definite disadvantage. They were under attack from both sides, pinned down.

This wasn't like an online game. This was far more

intense and more chaotic. Everything was happening with incredible speed and Jonah didn't know, couldn't guess, where the next threat to his life would come from. He couldn't defend himself in any meaningful way, except by keeping his head down low and hoping that the bullets would miss him.

And by not doing anything stupid.

He heard an excited whoop as L.G. broke cover and ran past him. Jonah caught his breath, yelling after him, 'No, don't!'

But L.G. was either too caught up in the frenzy to hear him, or too committed to killing the Millennials to listen. He charged into the fray, firing his pistol as he dived and rolled across the street.

L.G. had probably seen the manoeuvre in an immersive movie – but just as probably, he had never tried it himself before. His bullets flew wide of their marks, and Jonah ducked from a dangerously close ricochet.

When Jonah lifted his head again, he saw that L.G. came up a metre short of the opposite corner, leaving him on his hands and knees out in the open. He was an easy target. Jonah fired three shots of covering fire, hoping that L.G. would retreat, but instead he held his ground, firing until his pistol clicked empty.

'Get down!' Jonah shouted. But it was too late.

Jonah watched helplessly as Millennial bullets made L.G. thrash like a puppet with its strings in a knot. And then he collapsed, dead.

While the Millennials were focused on an easy target, however, Sam's team fired indiscriminately.

Another Millennial sprawled face-first into the dusty road. The other four had obviously concluded that they were now fighting a losing battle and threw down their weapons, raising their hands in surrender.

Susan fired two more shots anyway, which fortunately missed their targets. Jonah snatched the pistol from her. She was hyperventilating and her eyes were filled with panic and rage. Jonah pressed down on her shoulders, looking into her eyes – like his mum had done for him whenever he'd had a panic attack. It took Jonah a minute to calm her down, to get her breathing steadily again.

He knew exactly how she felt.

Jonah tallied up the death toll of the battle:

Four Millennials dead. Four wounded, including the girl that Jonah had shot. Two Guardians killed – L.G. and Anders – and Kasper limping with a bullet in his left quad. Six Guardians victorious, with eight prisoners.

Sam produced a coil of rope from her rucksack and began to pay it out. Her datapad chimed from her rucksack. Was it the signal from Jez to converge on the Old City?

'Here.' Sam had read the message and was passing

the rope to Connor. 'Get these eight under cover and tie them up.' Then she turned to Jonah and tilted her head, beckoning him to follow her around the corner.

'What is it?' Jonah worried.

'It's your dad,' she said, pulling Jonah close. 'He's been shot.'

Jonah seized up. His father had already died once. Wasn't that enough?

'Is he——?'

'He's alive, but badly hurt.'

'Where?'

'The message doesn't say,' Sam said.

'Where is he?'

'Jonah, no,' said Sam. 'That's out of the question.'

'WHERE IS HE?' Jonah shouted. Sam placed her hand over Jonah's mouth, begging him to keep quiet. She was right, there still could be rogue Millennials roaming these back streets.

'He's with Axel,' Sam sighed, taking her hand from his face. 'They'll be at Plaza de la Catedral.' Jonah had studied the map of Havana on the barge, and knew the plaza was nine blocks east and nine blocks north, through the old city. The area was still a warzone, but Jonah wasn't going to stay on the outskirts while his father bled to death. He tucked his pistol into the back of his waistband and ran.

15

Jonah rushed across the grounds of the capitol building and through the Parque Central, Havana's answer to Central Park. As Jonah ran, he recalled the times he and Jason had played football together in New York's Central Park. They were under military supervision, of course, but Lori had allowed Jason a one-hour visitation each day; something Jonah cherished as they kicked the ball between them and made up for lost time. Time, Jonah feared, that was finally about to run out on his father.

The streets appeared abandoned, but Jonah could hear pistol gunshots and machine-gunfire throughout the old city. Despite being the oldest part of the Cuban capital, Old Havana was the most intact. Its elaborate sixteenth-century Spanish palaces and domed churches had survived the civil war unscathed, physically at least, because the Americans had used toxic nerve gas to kill off the Castro loyalists. Thousands were killed in this neighbourhood, without a single shot being fired. But of course, the insurgents had poured in from the countryside, armed by Russia with heavy weapons and eventually radioactive material. And now it was seeing battle once again.

Jonah rushed east down a short street called San Juan de Dios that ended at a T-junction with a small park to his left. He needed to go north one more block and east two more to reach his dad. But as he raced past the park, two men sprang out of nowhere and tackled him to the ground.

He hit his head against the pavement but when he tried to raise it, one of the two dark figures pressed his forehead down while the other pinned him with one knee.

'Guardian or Millennial?' asked the black-painted face hovering over him. Jonah couldn't see enough of the man to assess whose side he was on: Guardian or Millennial. The wrong answer was going to get Jonah killed.

'Guardians!' called Sam's voice. But from where?

'On the ground, now!' shouted the man digging his knee into Jonah's stomach.

'Sam Kavanaugh, platoon leader for Sector Sixteen,' she said calmly, lowering herself to the ground. 'And that's Jonah Delacroix.'

The weight lifted from Jonah's head and body and the two men helped Jonah roughly to his feet. 'You're a long way from Sixteen,' said the man who'd held Jonah's head. 'I'm Crowan and this is Lukas, and you're in Sector Five now.'

'My dad,' Jonah panted to explain. 'He's been shot, he's at the cathedral.'

'He's the Uploaded, ain't he?' asked Lukas. Jonah nodded, urgently wanting to continue.

'Is it clear up ahead?' asked Sam.

'Depends on your definition of clear,' said Crowan. 'We've taken the cathedral, but there are Millennials scattered around, trying to pick us off.'

'Sam, it's only two blocks away,' said Jonah.

'Then you're not going alone,' she declared.

They left Crowan and Lukas behind and snuck down the Empedrado, towards the dark silhouette of the cathedral. A barrier had already been erected and a makeshift checkpoint set up on the steps of the towering church. Jonah and Sam knew to identify themselves before getting too close.

'Guardians!' called Jonah. 'Friendly!'

'Samantha Kavanaugh and Jonah Delacroix, from Sector Sixteen,' shouted Sam.

'Sam?' called Axel. 'Let them through. Let them through!'

A Guardian soldier raised the gate and ushered Sam and Jonah through the fence. The first thing Jonah noticed was a pile of bodies at the base of the church. He didn't know if they were Guardian or Millennial, or both. He hoped that his father wasn't among them.

Axel scooped up Sam in a hug and Jonah thought he saw tears welling in Axel's eyes. Jonah wasn't used to seeing that kind of emotion from Axel, but realised that until now, Axel wouldn't have known if Sam had survived the assault. 'I'm so glad you're safe,' he said. 'But you shouldn't have come.'

'He wasn't staying put,' said Sam, nodding to Jonah. 'And I wasn't letting him come alone.'

Axel looked at Jonah and his eyes hardened. Jonah recognised the look of disapproval, the look showing he didn't forgive Jonah for putting his daughter in danger. Jonah was getting used to that look.

'Jason's this way,' Axel said, leading Jonah and Sam through the arched doors of the grand cathedral.

The church was stacked with servers, at least three storeys tall. There was a hum that reverberated off the vaulted ceiling, making the building feel alive. At least a dozen Guardians were frantically rewiring the server towers.

'Where is he?' Jonah asked. 'Is he...alive?'

Axel gave Jonah a subdued nod, beckoning him down the aisle. The three of them walked down the long aisle towards the altar. Finally, Jonah saw his father, lying face-up on the long marble table. A young medic – Jonah guessed she was only a year or two older than him – tended to the bloody wound on Jason's abdomen. She riffled through her medi-kit for supplies.

'Hiya, Jonah,' Jason said, straining to lift his head.

'Oh, Dad,' Jonah said. He tried to avoid looking at

the blood, but it was trickling off the altar and pooling on the floor.

'It's OK, I'll be fine.'

'I thought I'd lost you again.'

'The body's a bit banged up,' he said, spitting blood. 'But I could always—'

'Don't say that, Dad,' Jonah whispered. 'Not here. Not even joking.' Jonah realised that his father was OK as long as his mind was intact. The body he inhabited was wounded, but would Jason really usurp another living avatar to outlive this injury, to potentially live forever? To be immortal?

'I'm going to get you out of here; we've got to fix your…to fix Luke's body. But we can't do it here.'

The medic returned with fresh bandages and pushed Jonah aside. 'I need to get the bullet out,' she stated. 'But he needs proper medical care or else…'

Or else.

Jonah noticed Axel standing in the aisle and moved down to the last step to be eye to eye with him. 'What's the first boat out of here?' Jonah asked. He wanted to get his father proper medical care, and there was only one place that would give Jason Delacroix, in the body of Lucky Luke Wexler, the medical care he needed: Manhattan. Even imprisoned by Lori, at least he'd survive. If they stayed here, Jonah was convinced he'd die.

'Easy, the data-barge. It's in the harbour now and

the transfer is under way,' Axel said, pointing to wires and cables sucking the data out of the servers. 'As soon as we have uplink, Tiller's taking it to sea.'

'Can we get on that boat too? With my dad?'

'What are you thinking, Jonah?'

'As soon as we get within helicopter range, I can ask Lori to collect my dad, get him back to Manhattan and patch him up in their hospitals. They're the best in the world.'

'And put him back in prison?' whispered Axel, restraining a shout.

'If we don't fix Luke's body, I think Jason will try to usurp someone else before it expires.'

'Disposable bodies,' Axel said. 'Oh my God.'

'And if that happens there can only be one outcome,' Jonah said. 'The living will declare war on the dead.' The living were already scared, but Jonah knew that if they found out they could be used as disposable host bodies for the Uploaded to live forever, their fear would turn to rage.

'You're right,' said Axel. 'We can't let Luke's body die.'

16

Granger hated being woken in the middle of the night – and especially when it was for bad news. *These days*, he thought sourly, *it always seems to be bad news*.

He threw on a black sweatshirt and fixed his titanium legs to his stumps. The messenger, a girl about half Granger's age, didn't know if she should look away as Granger activated his cyber-kinetic legs.

'What do you mean they invaded Cuba?' Granger barked.

'Just as I said, sir,' stuttered the kid. 'We lost comms with Havana and just now got a pop-up from a Millennial who managed to slip away from the attack.'

'What I want to know is, why does this concern us? I gave the order to abandon Havana months ago, so why am I now hearing that we still have people there?'

'The data-mining operation, sir,' said the girl. She was short, slender and mousy, trembling under the force of Granger's fury like a cornstalk in the wind.

'What about it?' he growled.

'It…it never proceeded.'

'You're telling me my instructions weren't carried out? That the servers in Havana weren't decommissioned?'

'The micro-servers were scheduled to arrive there in—'

'That, in fact, the Guardians haven't just attacked an empty city as I planned for them to do, but are engaged in the process of *capturing the Eastern Corner*?'

Granger pushed past the girl. He needed some fresh air. He stomped up onto the deck, knowing that the girl would follow.

'We...we don't know they are *capturing* the Eastern Corner as such,' she prevaricated. 'Our position there—'

'—is undermanned and unprepared,' snapped Granger. 'I sent the reinforcements to the Northern Corner because Cuba was supposed to be abandoned.'

He strode up to the port rail and gripped it with both hands until his knuckles turned white. He took a deep, calming breath, before he said: 'What happened to my micro-servers?'

'It was the Floridians, sir,' said the girl. 'The pirates hijacked our first data-barge with the new micro-servers on board. They demanded a ransom but doubled it when they learned who the barge belonged to.'

'I remember,' said Granger. 'But that was two weeks ago. And I told you what I told them, that I don't deal with common criminals.'

'Yes, sir, you did. Which is why...'

'Why *what*?'

'Why the pirates sank the boat. I did fill out a report on the incident, sir, and of course I organised a replacement barge, but…'

'But?'

'The micro-servers, as you know, are a new design. Our factory couldn't supply them in the quantities we required. I had them increase production. They worked around the clock until… The new data-barge cleared the Panama Canal at dawn today.'

'A day too late,' concluded Granger.

'Yes, sir,' agreed the girl. 'What…what should we do? I can assemble our forces to take back—'

Granger cut her off. 'A waste of time. We know the Guardians have the designs for the new micro-servers. They're using my own plan against us. By this time tomorrow – by the time we could get an army to Havana – the Eastern Corner will be gone, aboard a Guardian boat. No, Havana is as good as lost. But they'll take the prize to sea, and that's where we'll sink them!'

Granger rounded on the girl. 'I want planes in the air and boats on the water,' he instructed, 'and I want them searching for that Guardian data-barge. Tell them to take no chances. Any boat within a day's sailing time of Cuba is to be treated as suspicious and, if it doesn't have Millennial clearance codes, sunk.'

The girl gaped at him. 'But sir, the Eastern Corner houses half a billion live users.'

'That's collateral damage. Relay my orders to the captain of this ship too. I want us turned around and headed back towards—'

'B-but, sir, all those users...'

'What's your name?'

'Vierra, sir.'

'Listen closely, Vierra, because people pay a lot of money to hear me speak. This. Is. A. War. And in a war, there are casualties. That is inevitable. Now, if you find comfort in blaming someone for those casualties, then focus your blame on the Guardians. Those anarchists have left me with no choice but to do this. They have taken the Southern and Western Corners from me and I will not let them take another. I would rather see the Eastern Corner at the bottom of the ocean than leave it in the hands of terrorists.'

'Y-yes, sir,' gulped Vierra.

'We will give the Guardians a chance to surrender. If they don't take it, then any blood shed will be on their conscience and on their hands.'

Jonah helped his father's borrowed body into the hammock.

'Ow,' Jason complained.

'Try not to move,' said Jonah, looking down at the bloody bandages covering Jason's abdomen.

'Where am I going to go?' Jason asked, half laughing and half grimacing, looking around the cramped stateroom of the data-barge.

Jonah hoped that they could get close enough to Manhattan to get Jason to a proper hospital. Jonah knew there were closer cities, but since the eastern states had descended into chaos when America collapsed, he knew it wasn't safe to attempt to port along the coastline. But Jason's question prompted another, more radical, idea. *Where am I going to go?* There was one place where Jason could go – back to the Metasphere. If Jason gave up Luke's body, at least his consciousness would be saved, preserved online. But then Jonah remembered that the Metasphere wasn't safe for the Uploaded any more, not with that monster squid sucking them up. But if Luke's body died, Jason's consciousness would die inside Luke's brain. Maybe, Jonah wondered, Jason would let Jonah extract him from Luke just before handing over the body to Lori's people.

Perhaps Jonah could store Jason's avatar in a closed system, safe from the squid. But to what end? To exist in an off-line world for the rest of his life? Or to wait for another avatar to usurp, so that he could be reborn into the real world? Jonah couldn't let that happen.

His head hurt with the possibilities, and the risks.

And then he heard the explosion.

17

Jonah lost his footing as the boat listed violently.

His first thought was GuerreVert, the eco-terrorist group that sank the Chang freighter when Jonah and Sam first sailed into Sydney Harbour. But then Jonah remembered that Captain Tiller had yesterday spotted a suspicious boat on the horizon. Pirates preyed on these waters.

'Stay here,' Jonah said, steadying himself. Jason flashed him a look, rolling his eyes. 'I know, I know, where else...'

Jonah rushed out of the stateroom and raced towards the deck hatch.

His heart was thumping in his ribcage as he hauled himself up through the hatch. Sam and Axel were flattened against the deck and Jonah caught sight of Captain Tiller on the bridge, motioning for Jonah to get down.

A whistle preceded a bright flash that momentarily blinded Jonah. He stumbled against the stacks of micro-servers, hidden under the green tarpaulin, and someone grabbed him, throwing him to the cold metal floor.

Sam stared at Jonah intensely, screaming in his ear

to: 'Stay down!'

Jonah pressed himself against the cold metal deck, peering out through a wastewater hole to see small boats zipping around the barge. Bullets whizzed over Jonah's head. The ship shook and a loud metallic clank echoed in Jonah's ears.

'The propeller,' mouthed Axel. Jonah was sure he was shouting, but he couldn't hear anything beyond the ringing in his ears. Axel made a snapping motion with his hands and Jonah understood. They had stopped the propeller. They were adrift and under attack.

Jonah looked out through the hole and caught sight of his attackers. They were scruffy, sunburnt, tattooed and battered. They looked more like a street gang than the pirates Jonah used to play in *High Seas IV*, one of his childhood favourite role-playing games.

Sam rose onto one knee and aimed her pistol over the guardrail. She hit three pirates. Two fell into the water and the third was tossed overboard by his own crew.

Axel crawled to the wastewater hole with an automatic weapon and sprayed the ocean with bullets. But the pirates fired back. The ship was riddled with dents and Jonah worried that the old steel hull might not be fully bulletproof.

'Throw over your weapons and prepare to be boarded!' called a tinny voice through a megaphone.

'We could hold them,' said Sam.

'But for how long?' asked Axel. 'There's at least fifty of them out there and only five of us. And Jason's not exactly fighting fit.'

'He'll die if we're taken hostage,' said Jonah.

'And we can't let them take the Eastern Corner,' added Sam, arguing to fight the pirates. 'There're half a billion users online.'

'Let me do the talking,' sighed Axel. 'And we'll try to get all of us out of this alive.'

The trio rose slowly. Jonah put his hands in the air. Sam and Axel made a slow, deliberate show of holding up their guns.

'Toss them over!' called the voice.

Sam shook her head in disbelief. 'I really like this pistol.'

'Then we'll get it back,' said Axel, safetying his semi-automatic and gently tossing it overboard, into a waiting boat below. Sam followed her father's lead and threw her pistol over, placing her hands on her head, humiliated and frustrated.

The water below fizzed and bubbled and at first Jonah thought a whale was about to surface. Of course, that was impossible: whales had been extinct since Jonah was a young boy. And yet, here was a dark blue sea creature coming up for air on the port side.

It wasn't until a round hatch opened on its curved back that Jonah realised it was a small submarine. *So that's how they tracked us.*

A tall, wiry man – Jonah guessed he was older than his dad – climbed out of the hatch. His skin was leathery and he wore a gold ring through his left eyebrow and a black bandana with a skull and crossbones pattern wrapped around his greying hair. *This man*, Jonah thought, *was at least trying to look like a pirate.*

A clank turned Jonah's attention to the starboard, where six heavily armed pirates, four men and two women, climbed up onto the deck. Jonah spotted six grappling hooks hanging off the railing. Two of the interlopers, a young man and an older woman, rushed to the wheelhouse and grabbed Captain Tiller at gunpoint. Four more pirates must have boarded from the aft, because they came running, automatic weapons in hand, alongside the stacks of micro-servers.

Jonah and the others were surrounded.

'On yer knees, the lot of ya,' commanded the older woman, who pushed Tiller down to the deck with the muzzle of her semi-automatic. 'And hands above yer heads.'

One of the men tore Sam's rucksack from her back, searched it and tossed it overboard.

'Hey,' protested Sam. 'That was a gift!'

But the leathery pirate from the submarine scaled the railing, holding Sam's rucksack. He threw it back at Sam. 'Here you go, girlie; don't say I never give you anything.'

'Who are you...*people*?' Ben demanded to know, indignantly.

'We're rocket scientists,' laughed the leathery pirate, clearly the leader of this gang. His crew chuckled along with him, but Jonah failed to see the humour.

'Please,' began Jonah. 'My father is injured and needs urgent medical care; we're on our way—'

'Shush, Jonah,' hissed Sam.

'What part of let *me* do the talking didn't you hear, Jonah?' added Axel.

'Hmmm,' mused the pirate leader. 'An injured man creates an incentive to negotiate.'

'Negotiate what?' asked Jonah.

'Your ransom,' said the pirate, matter-of-factly. 'My name's Howard O'Brien, but my hostages, in this case you, call me Uncle Howie.'

And then he laughed out loud to himself.

18

Jonah's knees ached from kneeling on the hard metal deck.

The pirates had lined up Sam, Axel, Ben and Jonah in a row, hands and feet tied. They'd mercifully agreed to leave Jason below under guard.

'Now that we're all comfortable,' started Howie, 'how about you tell me who you are, and who's going to pay the ransom?'

A sudden silence fell over Jonah and his fellow captives.

Tiller broke the stalemate. 'I own this ship, but I'm a one-man band,' he said, hate dripping from his every word. 'So don't expect some big company to cough up a ransom for—'

'What is the nature and destination of your cargo?'

Jonah caught Axel shooting Ben an urgent shake of the head. Howie's crew were tearing the tarpaulin sheets off the micro-servers.

'Computer parts,' said Ben.

'*Obsolete* computer parts,' added Axel.

'From Brazil to landfill in New Jersey,' lied Ben.

Howie flicked the safety catch off his weapon. 'Do you think this silly gold ring and bandana mean

I'm stupid?' Jonah was the first to shake his head. Underneath the pirate costume, he sensed Howie was intelligent and calculating. There was more to this man than just a high-seas criminal, but he couldn't figure out what it was.

'No one would waste biofuel shipping parts to landfill,' Howie said, striding past his captives to investigate the servers. 'And I know you didn't come from Brazil. You charged through our waters two nights ago, docked in Havana overnight, and I've been tracking you the whole time. And if these boxes are junk, then you won't mind if we just toss 'em overboard and call it a day?'

'No!' shouted Jonah. 'They're not junk, they're—'

Axel jumped in, building a lie on the foundation of Jonah's truth. 'We're delivering them to Manhattan.'

'What do reckon, Irene?' Howie called out to the older woman who had been examining the cargo.

'These beauts are brand new,' said Irene. 'And purring like kittens. I haven't seen hardware like this since…heck, I ain't never seen tech like this.'

'Aldrin,' shouted Howie to the younger man who had grabbed Captain Tiller, 'toss me your datapad!' The young man started to throw the datapad, hesitated, and walked it over, handing it to Howie. The pirate leader plugged it directly into one of the micro-servers.

'What do we do?' whispered Jonah to Axel and Sam.

'We hold tight,' replied Axel. 'And hope he doesn't find the—'

'Metasphere!' cried Howie. 'You're running the bloody Metasphere from these boxes!'

Aldrin flicked at the datapad, pulling up lines of code. 'There's over five hundred million live avatars running through these servers, Dad.'

Dad. Jonah started to piece together the relationships. Howie was the leader of this band, Irene his wife, and Aldrin their son. The others were extended family maybe, or just part of the gang. Jonah wasn't sure. Either way, these pirates had just found their treasure.

'Ha! I thought I'd snared five hostages,' said Howie. 'And instead I've got five hundred million.' He kneeled down in front of Jonah. 'Now, you look like the honest one of the group, so how about you tell Uncle Howie who you people are and what you're doing hauling the virtual world around in my waters?'

Jonah froze. He didn't want to tell the truth, but he didn't want to get caught in a lie.

'No? Don't wanna talk?' mocked Howie. 'Then maybe I should go below deck and put your daddy out of his misery?'

'We're Guardians,' said Jonah.

'Jonah!' hissed Axel.

'We took the Eastern Corner from Havana,' Jonah

134

continued. He wasn't going to do more to risk his father's life.

'Enough, Jonah!' spat Axel.

'Go on,' said Howie. 'Your honesty's keeping your ol' man alive.'

Jonah figured he'd be better off telling the pirate the truth than angering him with lies. 'And your son is right,' he confirmed. 'There's half a billion live users based in these servers and we need to keep them safe.'

Aldrin was awestruck. 'How did you get them?' he asked.

'We captured the original servers from the Millennials last night and transferred the data onto these micro-servers,' Jonah explained.

'Right under our noses,' laughed Howie. 'The Eastern Corner's been just ninety miles away all this time – and now it's ours. Maybe we should do some unplugging.'

'You can't!' urged Sam.

'Can't I?'

'You know what'll happen,' said Jonah, 'if you take those servers off-line. All of these avatars, stuck inside, disconnected from their bodies.' Jonah had seen it when Sam unplugged Axel on the sinking Chang freighter. Axel and Bradbury's avatars wandered the Metasphere, mindlessly, their real-world selves confined to comas until their online minds and physical bodies could be reunited.

'But their families will pay handsomely to have minds and bodies reunited. You've just given me the ultimate ransom demand… Jonah, is it?'

Jonah nodded.

'Well, Jonesy, you're officially Uncle Howie's favourite hostage.'

Howie turned to Irene and declared, 'Reney, get these servers off-line. We're going to hold an auction. We'll release each avatar back to its user once the appropriate ransom has been paid.'

'You can't take a quarter of the world hostage,' said Sam indignantly. 'Those avatars inside are innocent people.'

'Bad things happen to innocent people, girlie,' Howie said coldly. 'Especially round here.'

Jonah had an idea. It was a desperate one, but this was a desperate situation. Auctioning off half a billion avatars would take weeks, weeks his dad didn't have. He needed a doctor and the pirates needed a ransom; or at least they needed to believe they were going to get a ransom. If he could lure them into the Metasphere, Jonah could direct them to the place where the Uploaded lurked, waiting to prey on the living. And one of them was a doctor.

'Think about it,' said Jonah. 'It'll take too long. By the time you get started, Matthew Granger will have found us and blown us out of the water. If you want a ransom, clean and fast, then our supporters will pay it to free us and the Eastern Corner. But they'll only negotiate with me.'

'And where are these supporters?' asked Howie.

'They're in a very secret place in the Metasphere,' said Jonah, hoping desperately that Andrea would have messaged him her location by now. 'They're private people. Very private.'

'Well,' said Howie. 'They'd better get comfortable with company real quick. Because you're taking me to meet these moneybags.'

Jonah suppressed his smile. He was going to lead Howie and the pirates straight into the eagle's nest.

19

Jonah materialised in the restored ruins of ancient Rome.

The damage from the squid was long gone and the sector had been recoded just as it once was. But it was abandoned; no avatar was in sight.

'There's nobody here,' complained Howie. His avatar was a squat, greenish-grey alien with big black eyes in a bulbous head. Irene materialised as a pink tulip and Aldrin looked like an old fashioned astronaut with a reflective, spherical helmet mask.

Jonah scanned his message log, invisible to the others. Andrea had messaged and Jonah tried not to display his sense of relief. The message was short, but sufficient: IF YOU'RE SERIOUS ABOUT CURING US, WE'RE IN GEORGE'S CAVE. TAKE THE TENT.

'This way,' said Jonah, wiping away the message and leading the trio to the Roman tent where he hoped to take his unsuspecting pirates to the Uploaded.

But suddenly two new avatars appeared alongside them: Sam and Axel.

'What are you doing here?' asked Jonah. He didn't want Sam, or Axel, anywhere near the Uploaded because he knew Andrea's clan were hungry and angry.

'They plugged us in,' she said. 'Sorry.'

'For "*insurance*",' said Axel.

'Howie, these supporters only talk to me,' Jonah lied.

'They come along,' Howie insisted. 'Because at the first sign of trouble, my crew will rip the Ethernets right out of their spines.'

Jonah was stuck. He didn't want Sam and Axel inside with him, at risk from the Uploaded, but it seemed he couldn't get Howie and his family into the tent without them. His only hope was that when the time came to offer the pirates for usurping, he could protect Sam and Axel from the Uploaded's hunger.

'This way,' he sighed, floating through the empty Forum towards the red canvas tent. He opened the flaps and stepped in.

The interior had changed and Jonah stepped into a dark cave, lit only by floating candles. The Uploaded were huddled together, and seemed to be chanting. Andrea flew across the cave at once.

'Do you have the cure?' she asked.

'No,' said Jonah urgently. 'But I've brought you—'

'Life,' gasped Andrea, her beak expanding at the sight of the living avatars at the threshold.

Howie had already stepped in, flanked by his family, and was pulling Sam and Axel through. The alien realised immediately that he'd been led into a trap.

'Carter! Unplug the girl and her daddy!' he shouted, expecting to be monitored from the real world by his crew. But Jonah knew that as soon as they'd stepped into the tent, they had been redirected to another server, a far-off part of the Metasphere, and shrouded by a firewall. No one in the real world could see what was happening inside the cave.

The Uploaded surrounded the pirate trio, jaws widening. Jonah pulled Sam close to him, worried that they would pounce on her.

'Jonah,' asked Axel. 'What is this place?'

'My crew will slit your throat where you meta-trance,' said Howie, fuming with betrayal. But Jonah knew it was an empty threat from a desperate man.

'They can't see us in here, Uncle Howie,' said Jonah.

'Are you offering these avatars to us?' interrupted Andrea.

'Jonah?' repeated Axel. 'What are you doing?'

'I am offering these three,' said Jonah, 'and there are eight more on the boat. It's a start. A show of good faith. They're pirates and—'

The lizard, Leroy, sniffed Howie's alien avatar and said, 'They smell so alive!'

'They're yours on two conditions,' stated Jonah.

'Don't do this, Jonesy!' shouted Howie. 'Please,

we just wanted our ransom. Nobody was going to get hurt.'

'Tell that to my dad who's bleeding to death right now.'

'And I hardly think you're in any position to make demands, little alien,' said Andrea.

'First, George takes this one –' Jonah pointed to Howie's trembling alien avatar, '– to tend to my father in the real world. He's been shot and needs a doctor.'

The black seal nudged forward and looked down at Howie. 'You have my word, young Jonah. I'll help your father.'

Four Uploaded held Howie down, and he scowled at Jonah. He didn't say anything more.

'And second?' asked Andrea.

'Nobody touches Sam and Axel.'

Leroy slithered forth and elongated his tongue, licking Howie's slimy, bulbous head. 'Can I have this one?' Leroy, drooling, glanced at Andrea, an appeal in his eyes.

'No, he's for George,' said Jonah, realising that the situation was about to unravel.

Andrea nodded grimly.

Howie raised his slimy green arms to protect himself, but it was no use. The hungry lizard dislocated his jaw, opening his mouth impossibly wide, and pounced on Howie's avatar. He snapped his jaw shut and Howie was gone, ingested and usurped.

'No, Dad!' shouted Aldrin, but his cries were cut short as he was tackled by a starfish.

'I will help your father,' said George, looking at Axel's gryphon avatar. 'But I'll take your life to save a life.' Jonah didn't understand what he meant until it was too late.

'No!' shouted Sam, galloping to stop the seal. But two Uploaded, a llama and a snake, blocked her path and pinned her down.

'I'm sorry for this,' said George to Axel. The black seal followed the lizard's lead: he opened his jaw and swallowed Axel's gryphon in one gulp. 'Sweet life,' he exclaimed.

'Dad, no!!!' called Sam, trying to writhe free from the snake's constriction.

Leroy stood perfectly still, his consciousness fusing with Howie's mind. George, on the other hand, seemed to make he transition almost instantly and beamed with a smile. 'Andrea, you take the tulip.'

But Andrea shook her white, feathered head and generously extended her wing to the snake. The snake slithered forward and ingested Aldrin.

'My son!' shouted Irene.

Sam tried to wrestle free from the llama, but the snake, now full of Aldrin's life, slithered back and held her still.

'I feel alive!' said Leroy. 'I feel his life inside me, I can see his memories. He is a pirate, his name is…

Howard, no, Howie, O'Brien. He is the leader and they have a city of their own. They hold Miami Beach.'

'Then that is where we will go,' said Andrea, sizing up the trembling tulip.

'Keep your stinking beak away from me,' Irene warned, her green leaves shuddering with fear.

But Andrea motioned to another Uploaded, a badger. 'Lotti.'

The black and white animal leapt into the air and consumed Irene's tulip in one gulp. Lotti let out a long, satisfied sigh of relief like she had just finished a wonderful meal.

'She was for you,' said Jonah, putting himself between Andrea and Sam.

'She's such a pretty unicorn,' said Andrea.

'Jonah?' called Sam.

'When I was a little girl, we didn't have any money,' said Andrea. 'But my mother brought me home a toy one day; it was second-hand, something she bartered for, but to me it was the best present ever: a unicorn. And it was all mine.'

'Don't you dare,' said Jonah.

Suddenly the Uploaded sprang on Jonah, slamming him sideways and into the cold cave wall. A snarling scorpion pinned him to the wall. 'Don't touch her!' he warned, watching helplessly as the snake held Sam where she stood.

'When the bank took our house and everything

inside it,' Andrea continued, 'they wouldn't even let me keep my unicorn.'

Sam thrashed, throwing off the snake and the llama. She rose into the air to flee, but Andrea was quick. The bald eagle lifted above Sam, opened her beak, and usurped her in one motion.

'Get out of her avatar!' shouted Jonah, freeing himself by slipping down and through the scorpion's claws.

'Thank you, Jonah,' said Andrea, opening the portal back to ancient Rome. 'Thank you for bringing back my unicorn.'

The eagle flew out of the tent, followed by the lizard, the badger, the snake and the seal.

Andrea was flying for Sam's exit halo. Jonah chased and cannoned into her above the forum. 'Let her go!' He punched and pulled at her wings, but the other Uploaded, including the scorpion, had caught up to him and pulled Jonah off their leader. The scorpion gripped him in the sky, knocking his head from side to side with its stinger.

Jonah could only watch as the Uploaded crested over the empty Forum and the halos glowed in response, expecting their rightful owners to fly through.

'You're mine,' hissed the scorpion, opening its mouth and swallowing Jonah.

But Jonah showed no mercy in fighting off the

invading consciousness of the scorpion. As foreign memories and thoughts of a life lived, a soldier of two wars, attempted to bury themselves into the crevices of Jonah's mind, he deftly expelled them. His brain identified and assassinated the intruding thoughts. He beat back the interloper and threw off the avatar, leaving the scorpion reeling in the bright sky, broken and dazed.

The other Uploaded were rightfully wary of Jonah and kept their distance. Jonah chased after Andrea but he was too late. The escaping dead disappeared through their stolen exit halos to be reborn in the real world. Jonah had lost his best friend but he wasn't going to give up without a fight.

20

Jonah's senses shot back to him.

He emerged from the darkness and fought the queasy sensation rising in his stomach as he awoke in the real world. Jonah opened his eyes on the barge. He was still tied up.

He strained against his ropes, and managed to yank the DI cord from his back. Three pirates immediately rushed over to him and held him down firmly.

Beside him, Sam's eyelids fluttered. She let out a sickly groan. Her body's new occupant was overwhelmed by the sensations she was feeling. Andrea probably hadn't experienced the real world in a long, long time.

'Get out of there!' spat Jonah. 'Get out of Sam's body, now! Sam, if you're in there somewhere, you can fight it. Do you hear me? Fight back!'

'I'm sorry, Jonah,' said Sam. *No, not Sam...* 'Sam *can* hear you, but it's no use her fighting. I have control of her mind and body. I'm the driver; Sam is but a silent passenger. And I couldn't let her go now if I wanted to. I don't know how.'

'Yes, yes, you can,' insisted Jonah, recalling Erel Dias's program. 'There's a way. We have a program that can separate you from her, if you let it. You can take...'

Another pirate, so white he was nearly albino, stepped out of the wheelhouse. This man hadn't come with them to the cave and hadn't yet been usurped. Jonah lowered his voice, so the pale pirate wouldn't hear. 'You could take his body instead.'

'But like *this* body,' whispered Andrea. 'And by the way you're looking at me, I'm not the only one.'

Jonah could feel his cheeks glowing red. 'I don't know what you mean,' he mumbled.

'Besides,' continued Andrea, 'we can save *his* body for somebody else.' She was looking at the pirate outside the wheelhouse.

She turned to Howie/Leroy and said, 'Plug him in, quickly. And the other one down below.'

'No,' said Jonah. 'He's injured, George has to—'

Andrea put a finger to Sam's right temple, conjuring memories from her new, host brain. 'Forget the one below!' she called, turning back to Jonah. 'You didn't tell me your own father was one of *us*.'

Andrea, of course, now had access to Sam's memories. It had worked the same way for Jason when he had usurped Lucky Luke. For Jonah, this was a source of hope. It meant that Sam still existed, even if she had been pushed into a tiny corner of her own brain. It meant she could be brought back from this. As could Luke. As could anyone. Maybe there

147

was hope for people who'd been usurped. Jonah felt so conflicted. He desperately wanted to get Andrea out of Sam, but he clung onto his own father, alive in another man's body.

The three usurped pirates, Howie, Irene and Aldrin, looked suspiciously at Sam/Andrea.

'It's me, you idiots,' insisted Andrea to her followers inside the pirates' bodies. 'It's Andrea. Now, untie me!'

They cut her bonds with a knife, and Andrea stood and stretched and fully admired her new body for the first time. She straightened Sam's tight-fitting black tank top. 'About the same age I was when I... Uploaded,' she observed. 'Maybe a little younger, but fit and healthy.' She touched Sam's stomach. 'If a bit hungry. When was the last time you people had anything to eat?'

Howie called over the albino pirate from the wheelhouse, lying that he was needed in the Metasphere. Howie plugged him in and the young man meta-tranced out. Soon he would reawaken with someone else occupying his brain and his body. The Uploaded were going to take over the pirates by stealth.

'My dad,' pleaded Jonah. Time was running out for Jason. 'He's not well, he—'

'Since he is one of us, he will be tended to,' assured Andrea. 'George! Take the boy downstairs and see to his father. We keep him alive; he's just like us.'

'Thank you,' said Jonah.

'But whisper a word of warning to the others out there and we'll throw your daddy over for the sharks to finish.'

Jonah gulped. He knew she was serious. But what good would warning them do? Even if the other pirates believed him and mobilised against the Uploaded usurpers, he would only end up back where he started, with the pirates to deal with. And Sam would still be usurped.

Jonah bristled as Sam's hands untied him. He had failed to protect his friend. After everything they'd been through, after swearing to himself to look after her in the Metasphere and in Havana, her body was no longer her own because Jonah had failed to keep the dead from rising.

'Thank you,' he said to Andrea. For a brief moment, he thought he spotted a glimmer of recognition in Sam's eyes, proof that Sam was in there too. If she was, did she blame Jonah?

He tried to push the guilt out of his mind, stay focused on his father. He led George, in Axel's body, down the hatch to Jason's hammock.

'Jonah, thank God you're OK. Axel? What's going on up there?' Jason struggled to raise his head, but Axel calmly placed his hands on Jason, urging him to be still.

'Dad,' Jonah said with a heavy heart. 'This isn't Axel any more.'

'Be still, stranger, and I will do my best to heal you,' George said, examining Jason's wounds.

'Axel, what are you—'

'Be still,' said George, 'and do not speak.'

'Dad, that's not Axel.'

Jason's face, no, *Luke's face*, drained of colour. Jonah gasped, thinking that George had opened a vein in the wound, but it was just the shock of recognition; recognition of one usurper by another.

'Who are you in there?' Jason whispered through the pain.

'My name is, was, no, now *is* once again; George Calloway, Doctor George Calloway. I was a surgeon for thirty-three years before my wife and I Uploaded. And your son very bravely brought me back here to save your life.'

'In Axel's body?' Jason sputtered.

'Dad, I had to. You were going to die otherwise.'

'And he still might,' said George in Axel's voice. 'I need to get him to an operating room.'

Jonah sensed another presence. He turned around to see Andrea in the doorway.

'We're going to Miami,' she said. 'We're setting up a new society for our kind, and Leroy tells me they have a functioning infirmary there. It's not much, but it's better than here.'

'A new society?' asked Jason.

'Of our kind, Jason,' she said. 'A real-world Island

of the Uploaded. No, a city of the *Reborn*.'

'The Immortal,' whispered George.

'You're going to Miami to take over the rest of the pirates and their families?' realised Jonah. It was an invasion, an invasion of the dead.

'It's our time now,' said Andrea. 'We deserve our chance to live again, just like we'll honour your father's chance to live.'

The threat was clear. Jonah would have to cooperate or else they would kill, or at least not try to save, his father. He was stuck on this ghost ship, heading to an unsuspecting city full of real-world bodies ready to be usurped.

'They'll fight you,' said Jonah. 'They'll resist you.'

'No they won't,' countered Andrea. 'We look like them, returning from a successful hijacking. They won't suspect a thing until we plug them in. We'll take Miami Beach without a single shot being fired.'

Jonah knew nothing was that easy. These Uploaded might take Miami, feared Jonah, but then it was inevitable that battle lines would be drawn between the living and dead. He had created this new breed of Uploaded, conscious and hungry for life, and unless he wanted to risk his dad's new life, he was helpless to stop their invasion. But unless he stopped them somehow, no one would escape the war that was sure to follow.

The war between the living and dead.

21

Jonah slept fitfully through the night.

He woke at least twice from the pain in his shoulders caused by his hands having been tied up behind him in the hammock. Each time he was relieved to hear his father still breathing. When he did finally wake in the morning, he had lost feeling in his left arm, stuck underneath his body, and when it returned, it was painful with pins and needles as the blood rushed back into his limb. As he shifted his body awkwardly in the hammock, he realised that it was no longer swaying, and the hull no longer creaked with the gentle motion of the sea. There was only one explanation. The barge had reached its destination.

Jonah heard clumping footsteps on the deck plates above his head. What was happening up there? He had expected gunfire and screaming when they landed, but there was none of that. *'Without a single shot being fired,'* Andrea had promised.

Jonah had to assume that Miami Beach was being taken by stealth. By the time the pirates even knew they were being invaded, it would be too late. He felt trapped, helpless to warn the unsuspecting pirates who were going to become hosts to the Uploaded, but right now he was mostly concerned for his suffering father.

'Dad? Are you there?'

'Hanging in, Jonah,' came the reply.

His curtain was drawn back; George had returned with two scruffy-looking pirates holding a stretcher.

'We're taking your father to the infirmary. It's at fourteen hundred Alton. I promise you, Jonah, I will do my best to save his life.'

Jonah didn't know how much his promise was worth, but George seemed to mean it and it was all he had. Jonah nodded as the two men carefully lifted Jason up from the hammock and onto the stretcher.

'Take care of him,' said Jonah, reaching his hand out and grabbing his father's hand. They hooked their fingers together for a moment until the stretcher moved towards the door. Jonah watched his father disappear through the doorway, unsure if he'd ever see him again.

Jonah found Andrea on the deck of the barge. His wrists were still itching from the rope burns, but George had untied him kindly. The Uploaded had guessed, rightly, that Jonah wouldn't contemplate escape while they had his dad in surgery. Besides, where could he go?

The barge was grounded on a long, white beach, with the rest of the pirate boats stretched out alongside it. Howie's blue mini-sub lay beached on the sand too, on its side – like a stranded whale from one of Mr Peng's history lessons.

The sand was bordered by tropical trees and low art deco buildings, which in turn were overlooked by hollowed-out glass towers. 'I always wanted to come here,' said Andrea. 'It used to be a resort town, a playground for the rich – I read about it in digizines.'

'It doesn't look like much,' said Jonah, noticing that many of the white buildings were burned out, abandoned. Many of the glass towers down the coast were missing panels, the wind blowing right through the skyscrapers. It was a beleaguered relic of a once vibrant beachside playground. It reminded Jonah of Santa Monica, the California seaside town where Sam and Jonah had been captured by the Lakers gang. They'd made it out of that situation by playing their captors off against each other. Jonah wondered if there was a similar angle here. But he feared the Uploaded were too united in their quest for rebirth to be divided.

'The Eastern Corner will be safe here,' said Andrea. 'Miami Beach is a strip of land – a barrier island – parallel to the Florida coast. When the pirates took it over, they destroyed the causeways that led to the mainland. You can only get here by boat or plane now.'

'Easy to defend,' said Jonah.

'– should the Guardians attempt a rescue, or should Matthew Granger attempt to get his Corner back,' Andrea finished.

The beach was full of people, sunbathing, swimming, playing. Jonah recognised some – the pirates – but there were many more. Lots were children.

'Are all these people…?' he asked. 'Have they all already been…?'

Andrea nodded. 'They're *our* people now.'

'Uploaded,' said Jonah. 'Usurpers.'

'*Reborn.*'

Andrea jumped down from the barge, her feet – Sam's feet – sinking into the white sand. She held her hand out for Jonah to follow.

'Soon, there will be even more of us,' boasted Andrea as they walked. 'I am spreading the word that this place is our new home in the real world. We have declared independence from the living, and invited Reborn everywhere to join us. We even have extra bodies available for the Uploaded still trapped inside the Metasphere, so they can—'

'Prisoners, you mean?' cried Jonah. 'You're holding prisoners so your friends can usurp them?'

Andrea halted, rounded on him. 'Why should I feel pity for the living?' she snapped. 'For the ones who persecuted us? For the ones who took my Mark away from me!'

'I'm sorry,' said Jonah quietly, assuming that Mark had been taken to the Camp or sucked away by the squid. He didn't want to ask her more about Mark, he could read on Sam's face that it was a painful topic.

They walked across the sand in silence until Andrea said, 'I still remember you from the Island. The "saviour". Most of us do, you know. We still remember how you led us into the light, to the salvation of the Changsphere. And then you saved us again, by bringing us the chance to be reborn. Because of this, I have decided that you can stay with us, to live among us; on one condition.'

'What's that?'

'That you accept us as we are,' said Andrea. 'Just that, no more.'

A beach ball flew at Jonah and almost hit him in the head. A little girl came running after it, flashing him a winsome grin as she passed. Jonah smiled back at her, but felt the smile freezing on his face.

The 'little girl' was not what she seemed. Her appearance, her life, had been stolen by someone else. Someone whose own life had been lived and lost. The same as had happened to all the people here, including Sam, Axel, Ben…and Lucky Luke.

Jonah looked at all the revellers on the beach – smiling, laughing, enjoying the feeling of the sun on their skin, of being alive in the real world – and a shudder ran through him. He couldn't do what Andrea asked of him. He couldn't accept that this, any of this, was right.

He needed to free his friends and he couldn't do that by living in a city of the dead.

22

It was a short walk to Jonah's new 'home': a flat on the tenth floor of a glass-fronted skyscraper called the Dorsal.

Of course, Jonah had no intention of playing house. But he didn't want to give Andrea any reason to be suspicious while he worked out a plan.

'This condo belonged to one of the pirates you shot,' Andrea said.

Jonah shivered as he walked into the basic home. He could tell it had once been a luxury residence, the type of home he'd only seen on vlogs of the rich and famous, but now what little furnishings were left were old and battered. The wallpaper was peeling and mould had taken hold in every corner of every room.

Unsurprisingly, the kitchen cupboards were empty. 'What about food?' asked Jonah.

'We have stockpiles—' Andrea began.

'You mean the pirates have stockpiles,' said Jonah.

Andrea glared at him, reminding Jonah of the promise he had made to her.

He mumbled an apology and she continued, 'We have enough food stockpiled to see us through a week or two.'

'And then?'

'We have the boats,' said Andrea, 'and access to our hosts' skills and knowledge. We'll provide for ourselves in the same way they did.'

'By piracy, you mean,' said Jonah.

'Unless you know a better way?'

Jonah didn't, and he shook his head, trying not to look at Sam. Seeing her like this reminded him of how he'd failed, how he had let her be stolen.

'Tonight, Jonah,' continued Andrea, 'we celebrate our independence with a cookout on the beach. Tomorrow, we send out the boats. I will make sure your pistol is returned to you, so you can—'

'You want me to be a pirate? I...I don't think I could.'

'Everyone will do their part in the new order,' she said firmly. Then, suddenly, her expression softened and she added, 'Samantha doesn't blame you.'

Jonah blinked and then stared at her. He was half convinced he must have misheard her.

'Havana,' said Andrea. 'You think Sam blames you because you couldn't kill your enemy, but she doesn't. She blames herself. She thinks she shouldn't have put you in that situation. She...wanted you to know that.'

Jonah swallowed. 'Stop it! Stop reading Sam's mind! You've no right!'

'Samantha's mind is my mind now,' said Andrea.

'Her memories are my memories. And she's right; you're not a fighter. Not like her.'

Jonah gazed into Sam's eyes, hoping to look through Andrea's occupying consciousness and find his friend again. But it was only Andrea staring back.

'Jonah,' said Andrea in Sam's assured voice. 'I told you the one condition under which you may safely remain here. Accept us for who we are, not for who you'd like us to be.'

She pivoted on her heel and left. Jonah watched her go, his fists clenched, trembling with suppressed rage.

Later that evening, Jonah found his way inland to the white building at fourteen hundred Alton Road.

He paced outside of the long three-storey building, nervously waiting for news of his father. A faded sign hung over the locked double doors of the small hospital building. In the darkness, Jonah couldn't read its original lettering, but he could make out the spray-painted graffiti: INFIRMARY. He hoped that inside George was staying true to his word, and saving Jason's life; Luke's physical body.

Five blocks to the east, Jonah could hear the Reborn celebrating their new real-world selves with a party on the beach. When George finally emerged, Jonah tried to read the blank expression on Axel's face.

'He's recovering,' George said solemnly.

'Is he going to be OK?' asked Jonah, gulping down his worst fear.

'He's weak and he needs to rest,' replied George. 'But he's a fighter.'

Jonah could slowly feeling his anxiety slowly slip away. 'Can I see him?'

'He's asking for you,' smiled the doctor.

'Thank you…George.' For a moment, Jonah almost forgot it was George inside of Axel's body.

'Thank you, Jonah,' he replied. 'You gave me a new chance to see the real world once more. And you let me be a doctor again.'

It was only when George led Jonah inside that he realised the building wasn't a hospital at all, but an Uploading Centre. The lights flickered in the long corridor and Jonah looked into the dark rooms, places where people chose to kill themselves, often in the company of their loved ones, to go to the Island.

'I thought this was a hospital,' said Jonah, spooked by the paradox of a dead doctor using a temple of suicide to keep an Uploaded alive in the real world.

'The real hospital got bombed out years ago, but these pirates have kept this facility clean and well stocked. They must've hijacked medical supplies,' said George, nodding to the makeshift recovery room.

Jason lay on a mattress in a dark room stripped of most of its fittings.

'Dad,' Jonah cried, kneeling down beside him. 'How do you feel?'

'I'm fine,' he said, with a cringe. 'At least I will be. George says I need to be still to let the stitches heal.'

Jonah looked over to see George closing and locking the door. He kneeled down on the other side of his patient and said gravely, 'Jonah is not safe here.'

'Andrea said that I—'

'Forget what she said,' whispered George. 'She plans to Upload you, tonight.'

'I won't let her,' said Jason.

'You're in no condition to do anything,' said George, turning to Jonah, 'and you cannot stay.'

'I don't understand,' said Jonah. 'Why would Andrea lie?'

'The Reborn don't trust you — they want you to become one of them, one of *us*.'

'Jonah,' said Jason, clasping his son's hand. 'You have to get out of here, now.'

'Not without you, Dad.'

'Your father is in no danger, so long as he pledges his loyalty to Andrea. He is already one of us.'

'George, are there radios here, or Metasphere access?' asked Jason.

'Both, yes, but they'll be guarded by Andrea and Leroy. Your best bet for outbound communications is that boat we came in on.'

'Jonah, contact the Guardians,' said Jason. 'Get

them to put a boat close enough to shore for you to get to. Paddle out if you have to.'

'You must go,' said George, clear and firm. 'Andrea will come for you, and when she does, she'll Upload you in front of the entire city.'

Jonah didn't know what to believe. Andrea had promised him that he'd be safe if he simply accepted the Uploaded for who they were. But she was speaking through Sam and maybe Jonah believed her because the promise came in Sam's voice, a voice he trusted with his life. He didn't want to make the same mistake by blindly believing George's claim because it was delivered by Axel.

'Why would you help me?' asked Jonah. 'Why should I believe you?'

'Because I've seen enough death in my life, and I don't want more in my afterlife.'

'Go now, Jonah,' Jason urged.

'I don't want to leave you, Dad.'

Jonah rushed through his options. He could stay, hope for the best. If he got Uploaded, he swore to himself that he'd usurp the first avatar he could find and come back to Miami to rescue Sam. He could hide out in Miami, but that might put his dad at risk. Or he could flee to fight again.

'You have to go, and quickly!'

Jonah slipped out of the infirmary and skulked through the abandoned inland streets of Miami. The entire Reborn population was on the beach, celebrating, and Jonah wondered if they all knew of Andrea's plan to turn him into one of them. He felt incredibly alone: his father trapped in a broken body, Sam and Axel overtaken by the Uploaded, no longer in control over their bodies or minds, and the rest of the Guardians halfway to Canada by now. There was no one Jonah could turn to for help; no one to stop the Reborn.

But that wasn't true.

As much as Jonah didn't want to entertain the dangerous idea of allying himself with his enemy, there was one man who wanted to stop the Uploaded from usurping the living: Matthew Granger.

When Jonah found the beach, he slipped past the partying Reborn and snuck aboard the unguarded data-barge. He slipped under the tarpaulin, invisible to any Reborn who might have been patrolling the boat. Jonah opened one of the monitor panels and tapped in his message:

MG – THE UPLOADED HAVE GONE TOO FAR. MEET ME IN THE M/S. JONAH.

Jonah encrypted it and sent it. He heard two voices on the other side of the cover and stiffened.

'Andrea's going to turn the Saviour,' said a gravelly male voice.

'No one to save him now,' chuckled a woman's voice.

A message popped up, with short-cut coordinates.

Jonah hid himself between the rows of servers. He plugged himself in and lay down on the cold metal deck, ready to meta-trance. As he inserted the adaptor into place and clicked it twice to lock in, he felt the rush of data fill his brain.

Jonah opened his eyes to find himself sitting on the branch of a tall pinewood tree beside an enormous, familiar spider.

'What's changed your mind?' asked Granger's spider.

'They're harvesting the living,' said Jonah.

'It was only a matter of time,' said Granger. 'This is the inevitable outcome of giving the dead their consciousness.'

Jonah knew he was right, but didn't want to admit it to himself because it was he who opened up the portal to the Changsphere, granting the dead their desire for life.

'They have to be stopped,' said Jonah. 'They've taken...too much.'

'Harsh words for someone who's taken the Eastern Corner from me.'

'Liberated,' corrected Jonah.

'Semantics,' spat Granger. 'But let's not argue. You need something from me and I need something from you.'

'I'm in...Miami Beach,' admitted Jonah, recalling the painful lesson of never revealing your RWL, Real

World Location, to anyone in the Metasphere. He remembered how he naively gave away his RWL to an avatar at the Icarus that he thought was Axel. That avatar was a Millennial agent that unleashed three deadly Recyclers on a busy section of the Metasphere. But he couldn't allow himself to be clouded by memories, he needed help now and Matthew Granger was the enemy of his new enemy, the Reborn, and thus his only ally. 'The entire community has been usurped by Uploaded, reborn into the bodies of the pirates who live here.'

'And you need a way out?' guessed Granger. 'I'm not far off the Miami coastline. I'll move my ship close to you if you can slip out on a boat.'

'OK,' said Jonah. 'I'd better get paddling.'

Jonah jumped off the branch and hovered in the air in front of his exit halo.

'And Jonah,' added Granger. 'I'm glad you came to me.'

Jonah dived into the glowing golden ring. The digital world slipped away from him and Jonah found himself in the black netherworld between the digital and the real. In that moment, in neither one place nor another, he realised he'd just declared war on the dead.

23

Jonah rhythmically stroked the paddle, pushing the sea kayak over the rolling, moonlit waves of the Atlantic Ocean.

The bonfires of Miami were long behind him when he finally rested his aching shoulder muscles. Despite the warm ocean water, he was shivering and soaking wet. He'd been paddling for hours and was now alone in the sea, rising up and down on the swells. By now, he figured, Andrea and the Reborn would be tearing apart Miami, looking for him. It would only be a matter of time before they searched the water. But Jonah had size working to his advantage. His stolen blue sea kayak was so low in the water that he was obscured from the shoreline by each relentless wave. He only hoped that Granger found him before the sharks did.

He heard the boat before he saw it. When he did catch a glimpse of it, against the moonlight, the dark silhouette blocked out the stars that hung above the horizon. Jonah banged his oar on the hollow plastic hull, making enough noise to draw attention to himself. As the massive vessel slowed and pulled alongside him, he got his first full sighting of the boat.

It seemed as long as a skyscraper on its side and there was no mistaking the icon painted onto the dark hull, the looped 'M' of the Millennial Corporation. It was Granger's vessel.

A rope ladder plummeted down towards him and Jonah paddled to reach it. He squeezed himself out of the kayak and hoisted his exhausted body onto the ladder. With each rung, he climbed closer to his allying himself with his enemy.

When he finally reached the top, he pulled himself over the rail and collapsed onto the metal deck of the vast tanker. As he struggled to his feet, he saw two titanium legs clanking towards him on the grey steel deck.

'Welcome aboard the *Marin Avenger*,' said Matthew Granger, reaching his hand down to help Jonah up. 'I'm glad you're here; finally as my ally.'

They were flanked by four Millennials, in black combat fatigues, holding machine guns.

'Then why do I feel like a prisoner?' asked Jonah.

'I'd prefer you feel like a guest,' Granger said, waving off his soldiers. They stepped back, leaving Jonah alone with his enemy. 'And where are my manners? Jonah, you are drenched and probably haven't eaten in days. Please, come with me.'

Jonah stood still, wet from the ocean and, as Granger had rightly observed, starving hungry from lack of food and hours of paddling.

'That's a request,' said Granger. 'Not an order. My chef will whip up something warming and I'm sure you could use the nutrition.'

Jonah followed Granger below deck, down a long corridor to the galley. He had never seen so much fresh food in one place. Overflowing bowls of fresh fruit reflected the overhead lights. The chef, a small man wearing only white, was chopping foot-long orange cylinders, strange vegetables that Jonah had never seen before. Jonah stood there, his clothes dripping and his mouth watering, until one of the soldiers gave him a fresh set of clothes – identical black fatigues with the red Millennial logo embroidered on the left chest. Jonah balked at the uniform. It was one thing to ask Granger for help with the Uploaded, but another to put the Millennial symbol over his heart.

'I'm afraid that's all we have in your size,' said Granger. 'And you can't stay in those wet clothes. You'll catch your death.'

Jonah took the dry clothes, begrudgingly slipped into them in the nearby loo, and joined Granger in his dining room at a tall wooden table. Jonah sat at the only place set with a spoon, two forks, and noticeably, a knife.

Granger was good to his word; his personal chef had brought out a spread of fresh bread, fruit and grilled fish.

'Merci, Maurice,' said Granger, waving away his chef. 'I caught this one off the bow of the *Avenger* this morning,' boasted Granger. 'Kind of like you.'

Granger poured himself a large glass of blood-red wine. 'And they say there's no more fish in the sea!'

Jonah didn't want Granger's hospitality, only his help in stopping the rise of the Reborn, but he was too hungry to resist. He ripped open a piece of warm bread, sating his hunger with no regard for decorum but in full knowledge that with Granger, there was no such thing as a free lunch. Jonah tucked into the fish, practically inhaling the real protein. Granger sniffed his wine, closing his eyes as he took in the aroma. He sipped the dark red liquid and calmly said, 'My people say I should have killed you when I had the chance.'

Jonah put his bread down and looked around suspiciously. 'The Guardians say the same thing to me about you.'

'Now I have the chance,' said Granger.

Jonah eyed his knife, wondering if he would need to defend himself. Of course, if Granger's chef had poisoned his food, it might already be too late. He cursed himself for being so careless.

'But do not worry. And please, eat up. If I wanted you dead...' Granger stopped himself, turning to Jonah with a smile and taking another long, satisfying sip of wine. 'It is my fondest hope that you will join me. And now is the perfect time.'

'I'm not going to become a Millennial,' said Jonah, looking down at the emblem on his chest and suddenly losing his appetite.

'This metawar is a war of attrition,' said Granger. 'And I have history on my side, Jonah. Order has always prevailed over chaos. You should know that. But why drag out this fight? Why waste more lives fighting the march of history? With you here now, we can be better together. You know, I have thousands of followers, and a scouting system designed to find and recruit the brightest young minds, but they lack the one thing you have in spades: determination. This world is going to be saved by someone with enough *determination* to see through the inevitable.'

'I think freedom is inevitable,' said Jonah. 'And you're standing in the way of that.'

'That's where you're wrong. That's where your determination is misplaced, misguided, and mistaken. People don't want freedom, they want order. They want to know what will happen *before* it happens. They need, they *crave* the comfort that comes with knowing that tomorrow will basically be the same as today. You talk about freedom, but what you fight for is chaos. Freedom, democracy, user-generated systems; they are all flawed because they are not what people need. Look at where you just escaped from. Florida. It was free and democratic, and look what happened. It descended into a failed state overrun by lawless pirates.

The United States was once the land of the free and the home of the brave, and it collapsed under the weight of its own freedom. Isn't it time we learned that freedom and democracy only lead to downfall and destruction?'

'But that's the real world, the Metasphere's different—'

'I admire your optimism, Jonah, I really do. But optimism without experience is just naivety. If the Metasphere follows the real world, it'll eventually crash out just the same. It's our one chance, Jonah, to get it right. It's the place where humanity can have a future. A place where we can give people what they *need*, not what they want.'

Jonah caught himself nodding his head. He believed deeply that the Metasphere was special and worth saving. He believed that the online world offered him, and everyone else, an experience that the real world could never replicate. Did that make him believe in Granger's vision? He shook his head; Jonah wouldn't allow himself to be swayed by Granger's argument.

'I fight for a better future,' said Jonah.

'How's that working out for you?' mocked Granger. 'A Metasphere overrun by digital zombies, bent on taking the very life you claim to protect. You might not have liked that I controlled the Eastern Corner, but do you think you've improved the situation by turning it over to pirates?'

'I had to get my dad out of there,' Jonah defended.

'That's the flip side to your determination, Jonah: impatience. You were so impatient to save the Uploaded at Uluru that you led them to hunger for life again. And you were so impatient to get clear of Havana that you gambled with the lives of half a billion users when you tried to slip through pirate-infested waters. And then when you got caught, you let the Uploaded genie out of the bottle.'

'How do you know—?' Jonah began. Granger knew more than Jonah had told him.

'I keep tabs on you, Jonah, because even though I want you to join me, I also know there is much I must teach you.'

'And what's that?' asked Jonah, turning over in his head how Granger could have possibly known so much about what happened on the Guardian barge.

'Consequences. To think about the consequences of your actions. Or do I need to remind you who led the Uploaded into the Changsphere in the first place?'

'I was trying to save them! I...I didn't know—'

'That's a child's excuse!'

'I'm not a child.'

'And yet you act impulsively like one. You didn't *know* because you didn't *think*. You didn't think because you didn't want to calculate the consequences of your actions before you took them.'

'I *didn't* know. I didn't know that the Changsphere

would awaken their…their *hunger*. I had no choice—'

'You always have a choice.'

'The Island of the Uploaded—'

'—was imperilled by you, Jonah. Because you overtaxed the servers of the Southern Corner to get at me. You acted without thinking and the world suffered for it. You don't play the long game, do you?'

Jonah hated this. He hated talking to Granger, because he had a way of turning things around, of making Jonah feel like everything he knew was wrong.

'If you think I'm so stupid,' he said sullenly, 'then why do you want me working for you?'

'Not *for* me, Jonah.' Granger sat up straight on his stool. He took another satisfied sip of his wine and smiled the predator's smile that Jonah had come to loathe. 'I don't need another lackey. I've got thousands of people eager for me to tell them what to do.'

'What, then?'

'I'm looking for someone, Jonah, with the determination to *lead* the Millennials. To take my place when the time comes. An heir, if you will. I think that person could be you – if you let me help you.'

It was just as well that Jonah had stopped eating, or else he might have choked at that moment. He couldn't think of a single thing to say, but Granger didn't expect an answer.

'The first thing I need to teach you, of course,'

Granger said, 'is to stop thinking in the short term. Since you seem to have lost your appetite, I suggest we begin your apprenticeship now. Come with me, Jonah. I have something I want to show you.'

'What?' asked Jonah, suspicious and uncertain.

Granger smiled again. 'How to play the long game,' he said.

24

The white room at the end of the corridor must have been soundproofed, otherwise Jonah would have heard the screaming as he and Granger approached it.

The room was full of computer equipment, but there were also three black leather reclining chairs lined up against the wall. A bespectacled Japanese man was strapped to one of these chairs, and he was struggling fiercely – and loudly.

A younger, muscular, burly man was tightening the last strap around the prisoner's wrist. He pulled his chair into an upright position.

'Thank you, Yuri,' said Granger. 'You will stay for the demonstration, please. We may require your, ah, talents again.'

'Da,' said Yuri. Jonah recognised the word for 'Yes' in Russian. This man sounded like a deeper-voiced version of Dimitry, the renegade pirate who'd shuttled Jonah and the gang from Moscow to Shanghai, where he was apprehended by Mr Chang's security forces.

There was one other person in the white room: a slight man with a fine blond beard. Granger introduced him to Jonah as Rognald: 'A gifted protégé of mine who has been working on the Uploaded problem.'

Jonah thought Rognald looked tired. Tired and miserable.

'And this is Kenji,' said Granger. He indicated the prisoner. 'Kenji works at my virtual R&D lab, developing antivirus software. However, you cannot speak to Kenji because his mind and body have been taken over by a digital intruder.'

'*Reborn*,' said Jonah.

'Hijacked by the dead,' said Granger. 'I had Kenji's body flown here, along with several other of my people who have been usurped by the Uploaded. I needed test subjects. I am pleased to report the tests were one hundred per cent successful.'

'What tests?' asked Jonah.

'Watch and learn,' said Granger, holding out his palm for Rognald.

The blond scientist shuffled forward, looking like he was carrying a great weight on his shoulders. He gave one small orange pellet to Granger and another to Jonah. It was heavier than Jonah expected but gave slightly under the pressure of his thumb and forefinger, as if it were sculpted from gelatine.

Granger reached out to Yuri next, and took his pistol from him. He loaded the gelatinous pellet into the gun.

'No, don't!' Jonah called, flinching as Granger shot his prisoner in the chest.

* * *

Jason lay on the recovery bed, willing Luke's body to repair itself. George had said that the wound should heal naturally, now that the bullet was out and George had stopped the bleeding, but that he wasn't out of the woods yet.

Jason felt guilty for being thankful that George had usurped Axel. His best friend had always had steady hands and an unflinching ability to concentrate when he needed to. It was what made him a great fighter pilot, back when they flew to protect oil tankers. But now, the real Axel was gone and Jason was still alive in a borrowed body.

'Where is he?' shouted Andrea, barging into the room and staring into Jason's face.

Jason knew she meant Jonah, but stalled for time.

'Who?'

'Your son, the only living person who knows what's going on here.'

'He's not with you? I thought you were having a big party.'

Andrea pressed her hand on Jason's bandages.

'Owwww,' Jason said, unsuccessfully trying to hide his pain.

'Who did he tell?'

'I don't know.'

'Someone logged into the Metasphere using those micro-servers. Who did he tell?'

'I'd assume the Guardians.'

'Then how long do we have?'

'Before what?'

'An invasion.'

Jonah opened his eyes, bracing himself to see Kenji's limp and bloodied corpse.

But the gelatine bullet had struck its target and burst like a paint gun pellet. Kenji gaped down at the orange spatter on his chest in surprise.

Jonah ceased his struggles, and felt the giant Yuri's grip on him relaxing in turn.

'Did you really think,' said Granger to Jonah, 'I brought you here just to witness an execution?'

Jonah wasn't quite sure what he had thought. It was like Granger was playing some sick joke on him, and only he knew the punch line.

And it wasn't over yet.

The orange spatter was *moving*, like it was alive. It was crawling across Kenji's chest, gathering in its tendrils, contracting itself into a perfectly round orange pool. At the same time, the pool was sinking, seeping into the fabric of Kenji's black T-shirt.

Kenji looked afraid again. There was no trace of orange on his clothes any longer, and his body stiffened.

'What is that stuff? And what's it doing to him?' cried Jonah, as Kenji's eyes rolled back into his head until only their whites could be seen.

Kenji let out a groan of pain and fell unconscious.

'What you are observing,' boasted Granger, 'is an off-line extraction.'

'The extractor pellets,' said Rognald, 'contain billions of nanobytes, small enough to be absorbed through the pores of the skin and then carried to the brain in the bloodstream. Once the nanobytes reach the brain, they identify and extract the brainwave patterns of the usurper while leaving those of the host body untouched.'

'The process takes about two minutes,' said Granger. 'We should see the results in a little over thirty seconds.'

In fact, it took twice that long – but, finally, Kenji blinked open his eyes as if from a long sleep. He tried to stand but was still restrained. He settled for wriggling the fingers and toes of each hand and foot in turn – after which, a broad grin lit up his face.

'Granger-*sama*,' he cried, 'you have freed me. You have returned control of my body to me. Thank you, Granger-*sama*, thank you.'

'Is that it?' asked Jonah. 'Is he…?'

'His body and his mind have been restored,' said Granger. 'His life is his own again. He is, as you would put it, *free*.'

'What about the usurper?' asked Jonah. 'The Uploaded that was inside?'

Granger smiled. 'Show him, Yuri,' he said.

Yuri helped Kenji to sit up. He reached behind his back.

He produced a small orange sphere from Kenji's Direct Interface socket. He held it up for Granger and Jonah to inspect, then took the sphere to a computer server. He squished it against the DI port.

The orange gelatine-like substance seeped into the port, as it had seeped into Kenji's chest earlier. Granger turned on a monitor and waited.

The screen showed an empty room with white walls and pale green grid lines. There were no windows or doors; no way in or out. And yet, in the centre of that room, a shape was forming. As Jonah watched, fascinated, the shape pixelated itself into a small frog.

'Good morning,' said Granger.

The frog looked out of the screen. 'Where am I?' he asked. 'Where's the Island?'

'He can see us?' asked Jonah.

'Through a real-world meta-window,' confirmed Granger. 'You recall I showed you the technology in my R&D lab? And now it's ready to be rolled out across *my* part of the Metasphere in the next upgrade – that is, once I have dealt with certain other distractions.'

Jonah stepped up to the screen. He asked the frog, 'Do you know who you are?'

'It's been so long since I saw my nieces,' said the

frog. 'They'll be grown women now. Mary was getting married. I wonder how they're doing at school?'

Jonah turned back to Granger. 'He's confused,' he said.

'Yes, he is,' agreed Granger. 'But you've missed the important thing.'

The frog had turned away as if forgetting they were there. Granger rapped on the screen with his knuckles. 'You in there,' he said. 'How are you feeling?'

'I want to go back to the Island,' said the frog. 'I don't want to miss my nieces. They'll be grown women now.'

'Are you comfortable? You don't feel at all... *hungry?*'

'No, of course I'm not. Why would I be hungry? When can I go back to the Island?'

'Soon, my friend. Very soon.'

Granger turned off the monitor. 'Do you see?' he said to Jonah.

The avatar was confused, like Jonah's nan used to be on the Island; unaware of the passing of time. 'You've turned back the clock on the Uploaded. Put them back to the way they were before.'

'Before our problems began,' said Granger. 'Of course, I will work on lessening their confusion without reawakening their need for life. But for now, I trust you will agree, this is the best solution all round.'

'What about that squid? The one that destroyed all those avatars on the beach?'

'That was an unfortunate surge of power, but the Extractor squid is doing its job. Finding, hunting and collecting Uploaded and transferring them to the servers on this boat, to be then taken off-line.'

'Put in a white-walled virtual prison, you mean?' said Jonah.

'It is only a temporary home. When the time is right, I will code them a new Island and return them to the Metasphere.'

'But until then…' argued Jonah.

'Until then,' said Granger, 'the Uploaded are safe – and in their natural, confused states, they have no conception of the passing of time. I dare say they are a lot more comfortable than their fellows in the Guardians' concentration camp.'

'It's not a…' began Jonah, but his protest died in the face of a smirk and a raised eyebrow from Granger.

Granger indicated the door, and he and Jonah left the control centre. 'So,' he said as they strolled through the tanker's bowels, 'what do you think?'

'Think about what?' Jonah stalled.

'The long game,' said Granger. 'The Eastern Corner is in the hands of Uploaded usurpers, these so-called Reborn. We can allow them to keep it or we can wait for the Guardians to attempt to take it from them. Is that what you want, Jonah? For the Guardians to attack Miami Beach as they did Old Havana? How many lives do you think would be lost were that to happen?'

'Too many,' mumbled Jonah. 'The Reborn have guns and they'll defend their beach.'

'Or,' said Granger, 'there is the third option. I have a Millennial army on board this boat and my lab is producing thousands of extractor pellets. We take Miami Beach in a bloodless battle. Will you join us?'

Jonah felt a lump forming in his throat. *Fight with the Millennials?*

'It's the best option, Jonah. The Reborn won't be harmed and you can have Sam back by dawn.'

'How did you know?' Jonah looked at Granger sharply.

'It wasn't hard to guess,' continued Granger. 'The two of you are normally inseparable.'

'And you take the Eastern Corner?'

'It's mine,' declared Granger. 'I designed it. It was built with my money. And think about it, Jonah. Think about those other options. You caused this mess. I'm giving you the opportunity to finally clean it up.'

'To play the long game,' repeated Jonah.

They had reached the metal stairs that led up to the deck. 'I don't know,' said Jonah.

'Once the virtual world is safe from Uploaded, it can be safe *for* the Uploaded. But if word spreads that the Uploaded have taken thousands of living bodies, you know that the living will turn on the dead.'

Granger was right. If it carried on like this it was just a matter of time before the living and dead went to war. If Jonah could stop that from happening, stop the Reborn before they became a target, he could save them. And he could get Sam back.

But that would mean facing his father.

25

The Millennials were going to war, and Jonah was going to join them.

He watched as twenty motorised, black rubber dinghies were being lowered into the water from the *Marin Avenger*. Granger's army had gathered on the tanker's deck, and an angry man called Sander was assigning soldiers to platoons and each platoon to a boat.

It all felt unnervingly familiar to Jonah. And that was why Jonah had agreed to join the Millennials in the battle of the immortal. Granger had promised a bloodless war, but Jonah knew that the Reborn would not go without fighting for their lives. How long would it be before the Millennials swapped their orange pellets for lead bullets? If they were going to storm the beaches of Miami, a full marine assault on the Uploaded – Jonah's dad, and the bodies of Sam and Axel – Jonah wanted to be in the fight to get to them first. He had to protect them.

Granger put his hand on Jonah's shoulder, sending a sharp shiver down his spine. 'I'm glad you came to me, Jonah,' he said.

'What the Uploaded have done is wrong,' he said,

meaning it. 'I'll join the fight to free those bodies.'

Granger put an automatic pistol in Jonah's hand. It was heavier and higher spec than the one Sam had given him. 'There's twelve pellets in there,' he explained as he handed him two additional cartridges, 'and another twenty-four here. If you aim well, Jonah, before restocking, you can free thirty-six people; thirty-six hostages in their own bodies. That's what this battle is about: returning innocent, living people to their own bodies and reuniting them with their loved ones. The usurped are trapped by the Uploaded and you can set them *free*.'

Jonah checked the gun and the cartridges, ensuring that they were stocked with gelatine pellets and nothing else.

Granger called for Sander. 'Jonah is joining your platoon,' he commanded. 'Issue him with body armour and protect him on the beaches. He'll be a target for the Reborn, and they'll recognise him, but he's an essential asset to the Millennials.'

Sander bristled at the command, but nodded loyally and escorted Jonah to a group of eleven heavily armed Millennials on the deck.

'And Sander,' called Granger, 'keep in touch.'

Jonah noticed that Sander was wearing a small earpiece in his right ear.

A young woman called Helen fitted Jonah with a Kevlar body vest and said, 'Feels good, doesn't it?'

'It's really heavy,' said Jonah, causing her to laugh.

'Not the vest, kid,' she said with smile. She wore bright red lipstick even though her face was covered in camouflage paint. 'Fighting on the right side for a change. Welcome to the Millennials. We're glad to have you on our team.'

Jonah opened his mouth to correct her – he wasn't on her team – but Sander ordered their platoon into the boat.

Jonah followed the others as they belayed themselves down the hull of the *Avenger* and into the dinghy. Jonah noticed that it was made of the same bulletproof Kevlar as his vest. Jonah counted twenty dinghies altogether, each holding two platoons of twelve soldiers.

Jonah sat down between the enormous Russian, Yuri, and the slight woman, Helen. At last, Sander lowered himself into the dinghy.

'Remember,' said the platoon leader, 'everyone on that island is an enemy – and that means *everyone*. These Reborn have snatched the bodies of women and children, so no holding back. You shoot first and—'

'"Don't bother with questions later",' mocked Helen. 'Yes, Sander, dear, we were all at the briefing. You don't have to repeat everything Mr Granger said.'

'I'm just making sure everyone understands,' said Sander. 'We have lost too much this year. This is one battle we need to win!'

'Mr Granger says we will prevail,' said Yuri quietly, 'and I trust his judgement.'

The dinghy was fully crewed now, but something else was being lowered down to it. Grasping hands plucked the object from the sky and untied its ropes. It was a small rocket launcher, complete with a stand to steady it. Jonah watched in dismay as two Millennials set up the weapon in the dinghy's bow. 'Is that…?' he asked, anxiously. 'Does that fire extractor pellets too?'

The Millennials laughed at him.

'But Granger promised…' protested Jonah. No one was listening, and his words were drowned out anyway as Sander revved the engine.

Twenty dinghies hurtled toward Miami Beach. A couple of miles out, the Millennials killed their lights. In the moment before they did so, Jonah saw makeshift wooden barricades arranged across the beach ahead of them. The Uploaded knew they were coming.

'Ready the rockets,' Sander called to Yuri and Helen.

The Russian man inserted a small missile into the cylindrical launcher.

'We don't have to do this,' Jonah desperately protested. 'We have the extractor pellets.'

Helen laughed, clutching the ignition switch. 'Your naivety is adorable,' she said.

Sander raised his hand and swung it down. 'Fire,' he commanded.

'No!' Jonah cried, out, throwing himself at Helen and pinning her arms to her sides. But Yuri grabbed hold of Jonah and threw him back into his seat.

There were nineteen other dinghies, anyway, nineteen more rocket launchers, and Jonah couldn't have stopped them all. There was a series of deafening retorts, and the night sky turned to day in staccato flares.

'Pull that again, Guardian,' warned Sander, 'and I'll have him toss you overboard.'

A moment later, there were answering crumps and flashes on the beach, but not enough light for Jonah to make out anything more than confused silhouettes and mushrooming clouds of smoke.

Jonah heard the whistling of incoming missiles, more explosions – perilously close – and suddenly the Millennials were shouting, cursing.

The Reborn were firing back!

A tremendous wave rocked Jonah's dinghy so hard that he almost fell out. Helen flipped the ignition and the boat's rocket launched into the violent night sky. Jonah's heart sank. He had led the Millennials to Miami and their rockets were raining down on the Reborn. People were going to die tonight; hardly a 'bloodless battle'.

Jonah caught sight of Sander steering the boat,

riding out the turbulence. His face was lit up by a manic grin. It reminded Jonah of the face of L.G. in the seconds before he was killed.

'They've got the weapons,' gloated Sander, paraphrasing Granger again, 'but they don't know how to use 'em. They're missing us by miles!'

This seemed like a massive exaggeration to Jonah, but there was at least some truth in Sander's words. None of the dinghies – as far as he could tell – had been hit. The crew kept their heads down, just in case. The twenty boats maintained formation, barraging the approaching beach with rocket fire.

And then, strangely, the answering fire stopped completely. Jonah wondered if the Reborn had run out of ammunition, fallen back to regroup, decided to surrender, or something else altogether. Whatever the reason, it didn't make Jonah feel any safer.

A wave of smoke billowed out across the water, and the dinghies were engulfed in a cloud of it. Jonah tried to hold his breath, but the smoke was already in his lungs. For a horrible moment, he feared that it might be a chemical weapon. He clapped an arm across his face and tried to breathe through the fabric of his combat jacket. His eyes were watering but he was alive. He could just make out the dinghies to the left and right of him, but no others. What was happening?

The shore came as a surprise to Jonah. His dinghy

surfed the crest of a wave, then up and onto the sand where it grounded. The Millennials piled out of it before Jonah's stomach could settle. He had to find his dad and rescue Sam.

The Millennials split up into their platoons as they raced up the beach. Jonah held his pistol and kept close on Sander's heels. Yuri was right behind him; he wasn't sure where Helen was.

Jonah trampled the remains of a wooden barricade. He readied his pistol, scanning for the defending Reborn. He was relieved to find none, but knew that didn't mean much. He wished he knew where his dad was. And Sam, who wouldn't even have a say in what risks Andrea took with her body. Jonah didn't like to think about what could have already happened to her.

He heard gunfire but couldn't see the source of it. Suddenly, Sander cried out and jerked backwards, crashing into Jonah and sending them both sprawling.

'I...I've been shot,' he whimpered. 'I've been shot!'

Jonah dropped his pistol. He felt himself panicking. He squirmed out from beneath Sander, heedless of the gasps of pain he was causing. He grabbed his weapon and lay flat on his stomach in the sand. He looked for a target and noticed flashes of light ahead, through the smoke. The Reborn had snipers in the tops of the buildings on Ocean Drive.

Yuri had reached Sander, but Helen then

reappeared from nowhere and pushed past him. For the first time, her mask of smug superiority had slipped. She had turned pale and afraid. Helen knelt by the platoon leader, examined him, and her red lips twitched back into their familiar smirk. She dug a bullet out of Sander's vest and presented it to him. 'You big baby,' she said. 'It didn't even break your skin.'

'You try being shot some time,' Sander groaned. 'Even with the vest on…ow…I think I have cracked a rib.'

'He'll only slow us down like this,' said Yuri. 'We should find shelter for him.'

Helen agreed with him. The big Russian needed no help dragging Sander back to behind a palm tree, but Sander protested.

'No way am I lying down while you two take all the glory,' he said, straightening himself and preparing to rejoin the battle.

From the smoke-shrouded beach, Jonah still couldn't see much ahead, but he stayed low and crawled along the sand, hoping the smoke would mask his movements. The snipers tried to pick off the storming Millennials, and Jonah watched helplessly as one of Granger's soldiers fell. He took no pleasure in seeing someone die, even if it was the soldier of his supposed enemy.

The Millennial force was over two hundred strong

and most had already broken through to Ocean Drive. They seemed to have the Reborn on the run.

Jonah realised that the Guardian barge was missing. It had been beached on this very stretch of sand, but now it was gone.

The Reborn were expecting this attack, he told himself. *They would have – must have – moved the micro-servers out of harm's way. Otherwise…*

'Wait up, kid!'

It was Helen. She, Sander and Yuri had caught him up as he approached Ocean Drive.

'Just where are you going?' asked Sander.

'Trying to draw the sniper fire away from you,' Jonah lied.

The smoke was so thick that Jonah guessed the snipers were firing blind. But then the ground around them exploded in small puffs as bullets penetrated the sand.

It was chaos. It was noisy, bloody, terrifying and – above all – confusing chaos, with the very real possibility that when the dust settled there would be no winners, only losers. How could winners emerge from something as bad as this?

Jonah knew they were sitting ducks on the beach, but on the other side of Ocean Drive, between the buildings of South Beach, there were plenty of hiding spots for the Reborn to lie in wait. Venturing there could be fatal.

Then the sniper fire stopped and Jonah heard voices coming towards them.

'Fall back!' shouted Helen.

They ran back towards the cluster of palm trees to take cover.

Jonah counted four people approaching: two men, a teenaged girl and an older woman Jonah recognised as Irene. They were dressed in dark colours, their faces streaked with camouflaging paint. Two of them carried pistols. The girl appeared to be their leader, directing her comrades with a confidence and panache that Jonah envied. Her body was no more than eighteen, pretty, with long blond hair pulled back in a ponytail, but of course, it could've been anyone controlling her mind. She was focused on the sounds of gunfire to the north. She was trying to sneak up behind the other platoons, Jonah realised – but she had just crept across Helen's line of fire. In one motion, she took aim at the young girl and shot her in the back.

Jonah's eyed widened in shock. Helen shot him a smile with her ruby lips. 'Don't worry, kid, I'm packin' jelly beans.'

Yuri shot too and hit one of the men, the armed one. The other man fled. Sander shook and fired after him but missed. Irene, or rather the Reborn controlling Irene's body, made a grab for the fallen girl's gun. As her fingers closed around it, Jonah rushed her, pointing his pistol down at the pirate's body. Jonah knew that if she fired at this range, he would die. He owed it to Sam to stay alive.

I'm not killing this woman, Jonah told himself. *She's already dead; and no one deserves to be immortal.*

Before Irene could snatch up her gun, Jonah fired.

Irene's face gaped in shock as orange gelatine exploded across her chest. She dropped the gun and clasped her hands to the sticky mess. She looked so scared that Jonah wanted to comfort her. He wanted to explain to the Uploaded inside her, a badger called Lotti, Jonah recalled, to reassure her that she wasn't dying, not really. But he was stopped by a bullet exploding into the tree trunk above him.

Whatever Jonah wanted to do, the battle was still raging.

It was the armed man. He was still standing, still firing, even though he had taken pellets to his shoulder and stomach. Helen shot him again, between the eyes, and he was blinded, howling, finally sagging to his knees and falling forwards onto his face.

Yuri fired a final orange bullet in the back of the man's head.

'What's happening?' asked the blond teenager, stirring as she recovered. She was sitting up on the sand, bewildered. 'Where's the man that was inside my head?'

Yuri fumbled in the sand around her to find the

small orange sphere that had popped out of her DI socket.

'In here; our first prisoner,' he said, grinning. Yuri dropped the hardened sphere into his pocket.

Irene gave a violent shudder, then relaxed. Jonah slowly helped her to sit up and reached around her back, catching the sphere as it wriggled out of the hole in her back.

'Where did Lotti go?' she asked, confused and disoriented.

'You remember me?' Jonah asked. Irene nodded and put her arms around Jonah. 'This little sphere contains Lotti's consciousness,' he explained gently. 'We'll Upload it to a local server, where—'

'Sander, what are you doing?' asked Helen suspiciously.

Sander had hold of the Reborn man's pistol. He was counting the rounds in its magazine. The man was still unconscious, but slowly coming to.

Sander met Helen's gaze defiantly. 'You saw what happened,' he said. 'We nailed this guy, but he still got off four, five more shots before he dropped.'

'We all saw it,' said Helen.

'The extractor pellets are too slow! It's an unacceptable delay that could mean the difference between life and death for all of us.'

'What are you saying?' asked Helen.

Sander reached to his ear and switched off the

small earpiece he was wearing. 'I'm not firing jelly beans while these deadheads are firing lead. From now on, we match bullet for bullet.' Sander swapped out his magazine chamber of extractors and slapped in a new magazine from his cargo trouser pocket.

'No,' cried Jonah, 'you can't do that! Granger promised—'

'Granger ain't here,' said Sander, 'and if he were, he'd agree that—'

'The kid is right, Sander.' Helen pursed her lips. 'Mr Granger's instructions were clear and we should follow them.'

'Easy for him to give orders,' chided Sander, 'from the safety and comfort of the *Avenger*.'

Jonah was grateful to Helen, if a little surprised. *She's probably only supporting me to undermine Sander*, he thought. Jonah hadn't known Helen for very long, but he thought he had the measure of her.

'Aunt Irene? What's going on?' asked the newly awakened teenager.

'Get back to the water line, honey,' said Irene, 'away from the fighting.'

'That goes for all three of you,' said Helen.

The man, coming round, seemed happy with that. He put his arms around the girl and promised her that everything would be all right, that her father would be back soon. They kept their heads low and rushed towards the water.

'You too,' insisted Helen to Irene.

Irene, however, shook her head at Helen. 'Nah, I don't think so, missy.'

She stood up, brandishing the pistol she was still holding. Jonah noticed a skull and crossbones tattoo on her neck.

'They invaded our heads and our homes,' said Irene, 'so if you've got a way to kick them out of the bodies they stole, I want in!'

Irene opened up her pistol and held out her hand, asking for extractor pellets. Helen obliged, giving her a dozen or so. Irene stocked them into her magazine chamber, then turned to Sander and warned, 'But if *you* so much as toss a real bullet at one of my people, you'll be awfully sorry you woke me up.'

Sander holstered his lethal weapon and motioned to Irene. 'Then why don't you go first.'

When Irene turned around and started marching inland, Jonah noticed Sander dropping an orange sphere. It must have come from the last of the former Reborn, the man now escorting the girl back to the water line. Sander must have taken it along with the man's gun. *We can't leave that here*, thought Jonah, crouching down to pick it up.

But before he could reach the sphere, Sander stamped down hard. It burst like a tiny balloon and oozed orange liquid over the sand.

'What are you doing?' asked Jonah, horrified that

the Uploaded contained in the sphere had suddenly been crushed to death. That sphere contained a human life and Sander had squished it like a bug.

'Not taking prisoners,' replied Sander.

'*A bloodless battle*,' Matthew Granger had said. But how many other Sanders had he sent to fight it? These Millennials didn't care one bit what happened to the Uploaded.

As Sander joined the others, storming towards Ocean Drive, Jonah bent down and examined the burst ball, hoping to be able to put it back together. But it was irreparable, the orange liquid continuing to seep into the sand. A person's avatar code gone forever. Whoever was in that sphere thought they were immortal, and now they were lost forever. If they extracted his father, Jason would be just as vulnerable. He couldn't let Sander, or anyone like him, destroy his dad with one stomp.

A metre away from the orange mess, Jonah caught sight of the teenage girl's gun. She must've dropped it when Helen had shot her. Jonah scrambled over, picked it up and checked its cartridge: real bullets.

Jonah raced after his platoon. The smoke was thick and the snipers were still firing blindly. As Jonah caught up to Sander, he aimed the gun at the back of his head.

He was going to shoot him.

26

Jonah thought back to the last time he'd held a real gun with real bullets.

He remembered how he'd hesitated to kill the Millennial girl taking aim at Sam. He'd shot her in the shoulder and worried that his lack of killer instincts was his weakness. But now, at close range, he knew he could shoot Sander dead.

But should he?

Sander wouldn't hesitate to shoot real bullets at the Reborn, or crush more spheres. But Jonah had seen so much violence, so much killing, that as much as he wanted to kill Sander, as much as he yearned to kill him, he stopped himself. He wanted to be above that. He wanted to stop the downward spiral of murder and revenge that seemed to consume the Guardians and the Millennials. But that didn't mean he had to let Sander waltz into Miami and go on a killing spree.

Jonah ran ahead, flanking Sander to the right. When he was ten metres away, with enough visibility, he steadied his hands and fired at Sander's right leg.

'AHHHH!' the Millennial cried as he slumped into the sand.

'Sander's down!' called Helen. Yuri and Irene stopped and turned back.

'A sniper got him,' said Irene.

Sander was yelling, thrashing his arms in the sand. Yuri held him down and Jonah ran to him and crouched beside him. He slipped Sander's belt off and tied it tight around his bleeding leg.

'I've got morphine,' said Helen, preparing a small needle from the medi-kit in her black rucksack.

Jonah leaned over and whispered to Sander, 'You're welcome.'

'For what?' Sander screamed, clearly unable to deal with the pain.

'Not killing you.'

Sander's eyes widened, realising that it was Jonah who had shot him. The injured Millennial's eyes opened even further as Helen plunged the needle into his leg. A stupid smile spread across his face as the narcotic took effect.

'It's a great day for the beach,' he said in a silly slur. 'Who wants a picnic?'

'I'm taking you back to the boat,' said Helen. Yuri picked up Sander and, cautiously, they took their injured comrade back to the water, leaving Jonah and Irene alone on the dangerous sand.

'You're a good shot, kid,' said Irene.

Jonah wasn't sure what Irene had actually seen. The sky lit up and Jonah ducked for cover. A deafening thunder followed, but it was just that – thunder.

'What do you mean?' he asked, feigning innocence.

'You know exactly what I mean,' she said. 'You ever think about becoming a pirate? We could use a steady shot like you.'

'I don't want to kill,' Jonah said. 'But I won't stand by and let someone like Sander murder at will, either.'

'What *do* you want, sweetie?' asked Irene.

Jonah realised that Irene might have some remnant memories, echoes at least, of the Uploaded that had usurped her. She might be able to help. 'To free my friend and get my father out of this battle zone. There must be a command centre here. Do you know where Andrea is hiding?'

'She's with the Uploaded that stole my husband,' Irene said. 'I'll show you, but she won't be happy to see you.'

The heavens opened, and cold rain poured down over the beach.

'She won't,' said Jonah. He had an idea, a way out of this losing battle for the Uploaded. If he could convince the Reborn to extract themselves back to the Metasphere and then help them sneak out of Miami, Jonah could stop the bloodshed against the dead and unleash the newly freed pirates against the Millennials. He would need to convince the Reborn leader to lead the plan. 'But I'm her only way out of this mess.'

* * *

Granger paced the command centre aboard the *Avenger*. He watched onscreen as green dots spread across the virtual map of South Beach. Granger had a live GPS link to each Millennial soldier, and of the hundreds of beach-stormers he'd sent into battle, there were still eighty-two operational. Most were moving forward, as planned. But he noticed a cluster of three green dots retreating back to the shoreline.

With a flick of his fingers, he expanded those dots to reveal the profiles of Helen, Yuri and Sander.

'Sander, why are you retreating?' he demanded into his headset.

'To build sand castles,' came the reply.

'Sander, what is the status of—'

'He's hurt bad,' called Helen. 'Jonah gave him a tourniquet, but he's going to lose the leg.'

'Dump him and continue your advance,' ordered Granger. He didn't want two of his operatives to be out of the fight just because Sander had stupidly got himself shot.

'Negative, sir,' replied Helen. 'He needs medical attention and—'

'Dump him in a boat and return to battle. If he's still alive by the time you've taken the Corner, then I'll get him fixed up. That's your incentive to prevail.'

'Copy that,' she replied, 'sir.'

'Can we bring teddy bears to the picnic?' Granger heard Sander mumble before ending the call.

* * *

Jonah stood with Irene in the charred remains of the Miami Convention Center. Rain poured into the building from holes in the roof and Jonah shuddered – for a moment, the entire building came to life as it once was. It was a flash of memory left over from his father's avatar. Jason had been here once, years ago, for a pilots' convention. As Jonah looked at the burned walls and ripped-open roof, he could also see the fresh wallpaper and bright hanging lights that once welcomed visitors from all around the world.

Jonah and Irene had surrendered outside, allowing themselves to be captured by six armed Reborn, and demanded an audience with Andrea.

Inside, Sam's body waited for him. Jonah had prepared himself for it, but his stomach did a somersault at the sight of her all the same. *She's pulled Sam's hair back in a ponytail*, he noticed. *Sam wouldn't like that.*

In a corner of the dank building, Andrea held a wind-up torch and shone it in Jonah's face. It took him a moment, therefore, to make out the features of the people flanking her.

To Andrea's right was George, in Axel's body. Jonah wondered what, if anything, George had told Andrea about letting Jonah escape.

Leroy stood beside him in the form of the pirate leader, Howie. Jonah could tell from Irene's anxious expression that it was hard for her to face her occupied husband. She clearly missed him dearly.

To Andrea's left, Jonah recognised Captain Tiller, at least his body. He didn't know who controlled his mind, but whoever it was had exchanged Ben's polo neck and captain's cap for a ripped T-shirt and ragged baseball cap. And, next to Ben, Jonah's father. To Jonah's delight he looked fully recovered, standing tall and healthy, but his face looked angry and disappointed.

'Hello, Dad,' said Jonah, quietly.

'Son, how could you?' asked Jason. 'You led the Millennials to our doorstep?'

'I had to,' Jonah defended. 'This isn't right, any of it.'

'The city is overrun with Millennials and they're slaughtering our kind,' said George.

'But you know you can't beat them,' said Jonah.

Leroy bristled at this. 'Who says we can't? There are more of us than there are of them, and we're fighting for our lives. Our *new* lives.'

Jonah took a deep breath. He told himself to remain calm. He remembered how Granger always sounded so reasonable, how he argued his points with relentless logic. *That's what I have to do now*, he thought. *Everything depends on it!*

'The Millennials have a new weapon,' explained Jonah. 'It's called an Extractor pellet and it only takes seconds to rip the Uploaded out of a live body and migrate the avatar into this.' He took the orange sphere from his pocket and held it out.

'Once the Millennials push these spheres back into a server,' Jonah continued, 'the Uploaded inside gets sent straight into Granger's private prison. That is, if the Millennials don't destroy the spheres before they get back to their boats. I was on the front line and believe me when I tell you: there isn't a lot of Millennial support for saving these spheres.'

'He's right,' added Irene. 'One of them Millennial monsters squished a sphere into the sand, killing the poor sucker still stuck inside. I can't say I loved getting taken over by you lot, but Lotti, once she was inside my head she, well, how do I put it? She became a part of me and I don't want to see your kind slaughtered. And this Millennial assault force don't strike me as the takin' prisoners variety.'

'I want you to live on, but not like this,' said Jonah. 'If you stay in stolen bodies more armies will come for you. They will kill off any immortality you think you've achieved.'

'Then what should we do?' asked Andrea, speaking for the first time. 'If you really are our saviour, how are you going to save us this time?'

'I say we carry out our threat,' butted in Leroy. 'We warned the living what we would do if they came here. We should destroy the Eastern Corner.'

Jason spoke up: 'No. We've talked about this, Leroy, and we agreed—'

'What good would it do us?' added George. 'It wouldn't stop our attackers.'

'Then what?' howled Leroy, frustrated. 'We just surrender?'

'No,' said Jonah, 'absolutely not. Granger wouldn't show you any mercy. You can't fight, you can't surrender. But you can escape.'

'Retreat?' scoffed Leroy. 'Is that your big idea, kid?'

'There are over three thousand of us now. We don't have enough boats,' said Andrea, 'and I won't leave anyone behind.'

'We only need one boat,' said Jonah, 'and the Millennials wouldn't even notice we had slipped away.'

'Weren't you listening to me?' said Andrea. '*No one* gets left behind.'

'If you let me extract you, use the Dias Protocol, get you safely aboard the servers on the data-barge,' explained Jonah, 'I'll get you out of here…alive.'

'You want us to give up our bodies?' scoffed Andrea.

'Or risk getting killed in them, or extracted by Granger's orange pellets. That's the alternative.'

'We're Reborn,' argued Andrea. 'We—'

'Won't survive the night,' said Jonah.

All eyes looked to Irene. 'He's right, and you know it.'

'Then why are you here?' asked Leroy. Jonah noticed Irene struggling to confront her husband's body, just like he hated talking to Sam's body with Andrea inside it.

'Because if you give up these bodies, my pirates will keep the Millennials at bay long enough to make your escape. I bet that Howie is inside you; however far you've buried him to the back of his head, he's still in there and he's seen your life, your struggles. Just like I've seen Lotti's, and that's a special bond that I don't think no one can understand.'

'You can lead your people to a digital immortality,' said Jonah. 'Or you can die on the beach.'

'Jonah's right, it's the only way out of this,' said Jason at last. Jonah appreciated his dad backing him up, and mouthed 'thanks, Dad' to let him know it. 'And I'll go first.'

Jonah froze, finally straining to say, 'No, Dad, that's not part—'

'I've been Reborn the longest; if I don't do it, how do you expect any other Uploaded to give up their body?'

Jonah wanted to argue, wanted to tell his father that he'd make an exception, but Jason was right. He could set an example and show the rest that he wasn't afraid, that he believed in Jonah's plan enough to give up his stolen body.

'I'm not ready to lose you again, Dad,' Jonah whispered.

'You're not losing me, son,' said Jason. 'You're saving me; saving all of us.'

'I will agree to this plan on one condition,' Andrea said. 'I stay in this body to oversee the extraction and the evacuation.'

Jonah fumed at Andrea's stipulation. It wasn't fair that she would keep Sam's body while his dad gave up Luke's. But Jonah had been expecting it, and knew she wouldn't budge. He knew she felt a responsibility to shepherd her flock. She cared.

Jonah was conflicted, torn about what to do. He wanted Sam back, but he also wanted to get the Reborn, especially his father, to safety.

'OK,' agreed Jonah. 'But when this is all over, you give Sam back her body.'

Andrea smiled. '*When* this is all over, she's all yours.'

The Guardians' barge was tied up to the stub of a demolished causeway on the west side of the island. Well out of the way of the Millennial attack. Jonah leapt on board and immediately peeled back a sheet of green tarpaulin. He laid a hand on the stack of micro-servers underneath it, and felt them vibrating softly. He let out a sigh of relief.

The Eastern Corner was still safe!

Andrea had wasted no time once she had agreed to Jonah's plan. She had made a few calls on her radio, ordered a first wave of her people to meet her here. A few of the Reborn had already arrived, looking nervous and bewildered.

These were non-combatants, Jonah realised, many of them just Uploaded children who, by chance, had usurped the bodies of adult pirates. Andrea had had them hidden somewhere in the city.

Jason led them up onto the deck of the barge and explained that for the Dias Protocol to work, they would need to give up their stolen avatar willingly.

'You'll be in a white room,' Jonah added, trying to use language that the children – that everyone – would understand. 'And you will feel a pull, like someone is tugging on your clothes. Don't resist it, don't fight it. After a minute, there will be two of you in there and you'll be safe.'

The Uploaded inside Captain Tiller searched out all the DI cables and adaptors he could find, and began to plug the Reborn into the barge's computer, plugging himself in too. Irene joined them on deck. Jonah noticed Howie and Irene's son, Aldrin, slip a DI cable into his back and prepared to let the Dias Protocol separate usurper from host.

'I want to be here when my husband and son come back,' Irene said.

Leroy, in Howie's body, was still complaining. 'I

don't see why *I* should have to—' he grumbled.

Andrea interrupted him. 'You have to give up that body because it belongs to the pirates' leader and we need him onside for this plan to work. And,' she added sharply as Leroy began to mount another protest, 'because I'm making it an order.'

Soon they had assembled and plugged in twenty Reborn on the deck, including Jason.

'I'll see you on the other side,' Jason said.

'This isn't goodbye, Dad,' said Jonah, trying to convince himself. 'Is it?'

'Not at all, Jonah. I trust you to get us all out of here safely. I know you can do it.'

It was all up to Jonah. The afterlives of over three thousand Reborn would be in his hands.

He used an online datapad to find the Dias Protocol stored on a Guardian server. He opened the user interface, and the program found the first batch of twenty Reborn. It quickly mapped their brainwave patterns, locating two patterns for each avatar.

'Remember,' Jonah said, 'all of you, the program won't work if you don't let it. If you try to fight it… well, let's just say it won't be very—'

'If you fight it,' interrupted Jason, 'it will kill you.'

'Um, yeah. But there's nothing to worry about, really,' said Jonah. 'We're just sending you back to a safe, hidden place in the Metasphere, George's cave—'

'Margaret's cave,' corrected George, who was

helping the children with their DI cables.

'For a little while,' added Jonah. 'Until—'

'*Forever*, you mean,' grumbled Leroy. He made one final appeal to his leader. 'You don't really trust this traitor, do you?'

'Jonah's only ever tried to help us, despite the terrible things we have done to him and his friends,' said Andrea. 'I think he's trying to help us now. And I don't see any other option for us, do you?'

'But...but we'll be Uploaded again,' Leroy sulked. 'As good as dead.'

'Better than what Matthew Granger would do to us,' said Jason.

Jonah tapped the coordinates of the hidden cave into the program. He turned to Andrea for her final confirmation. She took a deep breath, closed her eyes and, resigned to the plan that would send her people from their usurped real-world bodies and back to the Metasphere, nodded to Jonah to proceed.

Irene kneeled over the inhabited bodies of Howie and Aldrin, holding their hands. Jonah looked at his father. Jason closed Lucky Luke's eyes, anticipating the pull into the program.

Jonah hovered his finger over the datapad and tapped twice on the pulsing red button: EXECUTE.

27

Jonah watched the twenty Reborn twitch in their meta-trance.

Behind their flickering eyelids, he knew that each of them was undergoing a confusing separation of mind and body. Andrea and George watched anxiously, ensuring Jonah was true to his word.

Jonah showed them the display on his datapad. The progress bars that tracked each avatar inched across the screen. On the monitor, Jonah watched each Uploaded avatar, confined to its own white room, finally separate from its usurped avatar. Once the extraction was complete, Jonah opened the portals, leading the Uploaded back to the secret cave. He felt burdened by the new responsibility of looking after these digital souls.

Next, Jonah sent pop-up messages to each living avatar, complete with auto-generated short cuts to their exit halos. One by one, the pirates on the deck started to wake up in their own bodies. They surveyed their surroundings, and narrowed their eyes in suspicion and anger as they pieced together what had happened to them.

'Howdy there, lil' pardner,' said Luke, looking at

Jonah in a daze. Jonah didn't know whether to expect relief or anger from Luke Wexler after everything he'd been subjected to. But the cowboy took it all in his casual stride. 'Whoa, what a wild ride,' he said, shaking off the effect of the usurping.

'I don't know how much you remember of the past two days,' Andrea said to her reawakened pirates.

Irene embraced her son, and then Howie. It was the pirate leader who spoke first. 'You can save the speech, sister,' he said as he clambered to his feet. Howie looked unsteady, but Irene held him up. Once he regained his posture, he looked every bit the fierce pirate Jonah had encountered on the high sea. He towered over Andrea in Sam's body. 'We know exactly what you did to us, and *you*...' He pointed angrily at Jonah. 'You're even worse than they are, because you fed us to these parasites!'

'And I'd do it again,' asserted Jonah, 'to save half a billion people. But the game has changed now and we have to work together.'

'Yeah, yeah, I know. You brought the Millennials to my island and now they're shooting up the place and none of us are safe.'

'But Jonah has a way out,' said George, still inhabiting Axel's body.

'I heard about that too. Oh, don't look so surprised, old man. I've been here all the time, a prisoner inside my own head, and I've been thinking about this escape plan of yours and I reckon, well...' Howie paused to draw breath, and Jonah stopped breathing altogether.

'I reckon Irene's right. It's the best chance we've got,' said Howie. 'For all of us.'

Finally, Jonah exhaled. He had staked everything on this, gambled on getting the Uploaded and the pirates to cooperate, and it had paid off. This time.

'So, yeah,' said Howie, 'you can count us in, me and my crew. We'll start by freeing the prisoners you took. Some of them know how to fight.'

Andrea nodded, also looking relieved. 'We'll pull the Reborn off the front lines, in groups of twenty at a time, and bring them back here for extraction while your people rotate into the battle.'

'And we'll keep those mangy Millennials pinned down while you sail outta here.'

'And the Eastern Corner?' asked Jonah.

'Take it,' said Howie. 'You were right, what you said at the start. Having those servers here can only bring us trouble.'

'We have a deal, then,' said Andrea. She held out her hand.

Howie eyed it for a moment, then took it. 'It's a deal,' he agreed. 'But don't think this means anything is forgotten or forgiven. By sunrise, this island will be ours again – and before that happens you'd best be a long, long way away from here. That goes for all of you, Reborn *and* Guardians. If we cross paths again…'

He left the unspoken threat hanging in the air.

It took just over five hours to extract all of the Uploaded from the pirates' bodies. Now Captain Tiller had his body back, he was able to produce a secret store of Ethernet cords and DI adaptors, allowing Jonah and Andrea to increase the extraction process to over three hundred pirates at a time. The Reborn didn't go without an argument, but they trusted their leaders and ultimately followed their commands. It was clearly important to them to stick together.

Jonah was relieved that Andrea was so convincing, persuading the Reborn to let the Dias Protocol work on them. But he was furious that she was still squatting in Sam's body, and worried that she wouldn't keep to her word. And he wasn't the only one.

When Jonah sent George into the Protocol, Axel woke up and immediately took a swing at Jonah. Luckily, Axel was still woozy from the adjustment of being in control of his own body, and was slower than normal. Jonah ducked, avoiding the punch.

'I know you're angry,' Jonah said.

'There isn't a word for what I am,' said Axel, his jaw clenched with rage.

'I'm sorry, but I did what I had to do to save my dad. I had no choice.'

'You always have a choice, Jonah!' shouted Axel. 'And choices have consequences.'

Jonah thought back to Granger's lecture to him, the one about not thinking through the consequences of his actions, of his choices.

'Dad would have died,' Jonah explained. He looked down at Axel's hands, the steady hands that when controlled by a skilled surgeon had saved Jason's life, in Luke's body. 'And I knew you could save him.'

'I know it's little consolation, pardner,' interrupted Luke. 'But I'm mighty thankful that you patched me up, even if you were doing it unwillingly, like.'

'I don't know if I'll ever forgive you,' Axel said to Jonah. 'But right now, I just want Sam back.'

'So do I,' said Jonah. 'But I made a deal with Andrea. If she's going to keep up her end, we need to do the same.'

'When this is all over,' threatened Axel, 'I get my daughter back or you…'

Axel steadied himself, glaring at Jonah, silencing his threat. Axel stormed off towards the aft of the barge.

'He'll calm down,' said Luke.

'You think?'

'You just get him his little girl back, and all will be forgiven,' said Luke. 'That's sure as shootin'.'

'I don't know.' Jonah wished he had Axel onside.

'Listen, your daddy hijacked my body for four

months, and I'm not exactly pleased as punch with being used as his personal passport back to the real world, but I think I got to know him. You get the measure of a man when he takes over your brain, and I gotta say, Jonah, he's awfully proud of you.'

'I'm sorry you were usurped,' said Jonah.

'Tell you what, Jonah. If we make it out of this alive, I'll make you a deal. You give me the rights to this skirmish for me to code into a new game, and we'll be even stevens. How does that sound?'

'You want to turn what happened to you into a video game?'

'Heck yeah! I may have not been in the driver's seat of my own head, but it's been the ride of my life.'

'OK, deal,' Jonah agreed quickly. He'd been half expecting fury from Luke. Instead, he realised that like Irene, the Texan came to sympathise with his usurper. He just hoped Sam would be so forgiving.

28

Jonah looked back at the fires of Miami.

The pirates were still fighting the Millennials, but Granger's forces were hopelessly outnumbered now and their orange ammunition was useless. It was only a matter of time before the invaders would be captured or killed by Howie's people. Jonah hoped the pirates would show some mercy towards the Millennials.

Once all the Reborn had been reloaded onto the micro-servers, Captain Tiller navigated the barge down the canal and slipped out unseen past Biscay Point. They headed south-east, towards the Bahamas. The storm of the night before had blown over and the morning sun was just starting to peek over the ocean, bathing the barge in a new light. But the new day was clouded by a promise yet to be fulfilled. Andrea was still in Sam's body.

'What about my little girl?' Axel said, glaring at his trapped daughter. 'Your kind are safely on board, hidden away in the Metasphere. It's time for you to join them and give me back my daughter!'

'You've got what you wanted,' said Andrea, standing her ground. She indicated the micro-servers. 'The Eastern Corner is in Guardian hands. The pirates have what they wanted too: their island back. That just leaves us, the Reborn.'

This was Jonah's chance. As Andrea and Axel were arguing, Jonah plucked the lone extractor pellet from his pocket and loaded it into his gun.

'Uploaded, not Reborn,' said Axel, pointedly.

'Exactly my point,' said Andrea. 'You promised you'd help my people, but they're right back where we started. They're hiding out in the Metasphere. So, I'll be staying right here in this body, in the real world.'

'No you won't,' said Jonah. Andrea turned, looking down the narrow barrel of Jonah's pistol. Jonah looked into Sam's stolen eyes, hoping to see a glimpse of his friend. And then he fired.

The extractor pellet hit Andrea just below her neck and she slammed backwards. Axel was quick; he grabbed his daughter's falling body before it hit the floor. Sam twitched and writhed. Jonah kneeled down, holding her close. The tiny orange nanobytes seeped into her skin and in minutes would expunge Andrea from Sam's brain.

Jonah and Axel shared a look, which Jonah interpreted as *thanks*, but could have also been blame.

'It's OK,' Jonah whispered to both Andrea and Sam.

But Andrea was slipping away and Sam was taking back her body. Jonah was going to get his best friend back.

Granger stomped along the deck of the *Marin Avenger*, shouting into his headset.

'Who is this? And how did you decrypt my private frequency?'

'*My name is Howie O'Brien*,' answered a taunting baritone voice. '*But my hostages, your army, can call me Uncle Howie.*'

'You're a Reborn?' spluttered Granger.

'*Not even close*,' said the radio voice. '*You'd call me a pirate, but I'd say I'm just being entrepreneurial. Kinda like you!*'

'So you're back in control over there?'

There were lights approaching across the dawn sea, and Granger could hear engines whining. The remnants of his invading force, those who'd escaped capture, were returning from Miami Beach.

'*The Guardians lit out a couple of hours ago*,' said O'Brien, '*with the former Reborn in tow and the Eastern Corner for good measure.*'

A familiar impotent rage was building in Granger's chest. 'You...you ignorant...' he bellowed. 'Why didn't you stop them? My soldiers were fighting to free you from those parasites. We're on the same side!'

'*Not when your people started shooting real bullets.*'

'What?' Granger's instructions had been crystal clear. He wanted the Uploaded captured and the bodies freed. He wanted, no, he needed, to be the saviour, the one person the world could rely on to safely excise the dead.

'Now, if you want to discuss a deal to get your people back, the negotiating table is open.'

Someone had come up behind Granger. He had failed to get his attention by clearing his throat, so now he tugged at Granger's elbow. 'Sir, please.'

It was Rognald. Granger covered the microphone and said, 'I'm busy.'

'But, Mr Granger, this is urgent!'

Granger brushed the bio-hacker away and stabbed at his radio's 'send' button. 'O'Brien! Are you still there?'

'Remember, that's Uncle Howie to my hostages,' came the response. *'By which I mean fifty-seven of your fighters. Shall we open the bidding at ten million?'*

'You need to see this, Mr Granger,' urged Rognald.

'And before you tell me you don't deal with common criminals, let me ask you this: How's that working out for you lately?'

Granger's force had the technological advantage. They should have taken Miami, picked off the Reborn one by one. How did it go so wrong?

'You need to see what's happening. In the Metasphere, sir.'

'You need to ask yourself, what's more important to you, skipper?'

'It's the Extractor squid, sir. It's…'

'*The money or the supporters. Because the former, we all know you're rolling in, but the latter...*'

'It's completely out of control!'

'*These days, I'd say you need all the support you can get. Make your mind up soon, Mr Granger, because the price goes up for every hour you—*'

'I'll come back to you,' he barked into the handset, and turned to Rognald. 'I pay you to keep control.'

29

Andrea's world went black, but only for a few seconds.

Then, the void in Andrea's mind was filled with dreams of smoke and fire and falling. She was in her Navy helicopter, wrestling with the controls as it spiralled down towards New York's Central Park. In one uncontrollable descent, it all slipped away: the life she'd started with Mark, the future they planned to have together. The altitude gauge burned into her mind as that imagined life evaporated and exploded when her helicopter hit the ground.

She opened her eyes and she was somewhere worse.

A huge, candlelit cave. Had she been here before? No, this was George's cave – 'Margaret's Cave'. It was supposed to be a safe place, a place to hide, but it felt like a prison.

Andrea could hear screaming, as if from a long way away.

She shrank into a corner, burying her face in her hands. *Hands? No…* She had no hands, only wings and talons. Her avatar was a bald eagle. Yes, of course it was. So why, for a moment there, had she imagined…?

Voices called her name.

There were two of them, hovering in the cave entrance. They looked torn between leaving and coming back for her. *Only two?* thought Andrea. *There should be more. There should be thousands.*

'What are you doing back here?' cried a black seal. Andrea knew his name, but she couldn't recall it. 'Andrea?'

'Never mind that,' snapped a lizard with a broad, flat head. 'We have to get out of this death trap. It's almost here!'

'No, look at her,' said the seal. 'There's something wrong with her. I think she's... Look, Leroy. Look in her eyes. Andrea's *confused*!'

The lizard snarled. 'They betrayed us, the Guardians. I knew they would. I said we shouldn't have trusted them. What did they do to you?'

The question was meant for Andrea, but she didn't know the answer. She didn't understand what was happening to her. She gaped up at the lizard, unable to answer his question.

'We don't have time for this,' said the lizard, and he turned to fly out of the cave.

Those screams were closer than Andrea had thought they were. They were coming from right outside.

'Leroy, no,' said the seal. 'We have to take Andrea with us.'

'What's the point? She's lost to us now; do you think...yes, they must've shot her with an extractor pellet instead. She'll only slow us down!'

'Leroy, you get back here this second!' barked the seal. 'Andrea's been good to us. I don't know where we'd be if it weren't for her, and we are not going to abandon her now. And if you try, so help me, I will spend the rest of my afterlife finding a way to depixelate you, you slimy lizard!'

The outburst left the seal breathless, but it worked.

The lizard sighed, resigned, and he and the seal flew back into the cave, to Andrea's side. They took her gently by the shoulders and lifted her off the ground.

'Where are we going?' asked Andrea, hopefully. 'To the Island?'

A look passed between her two escorts. Then the seal, George, said tenderly, 'Yes, Andrea. That's right. We are going to the Island.'

'Good,' said Andrea, and she smiled. 'I like the Island; Mark will be there.'

They were halfway to the cave entrance, a bright circle of blue sky, and Andrea was beginning to relax. She wasn't even sure now why she had been so upset. As soon as she was back on the Island, she thought, everything would be OK. Mark would be there and together they'd stroll on the sand, bathe in the warm waves, and fly together like they always had. Like they always would.

Then, a shadow passed over her, and her escorts froze in fright.

Something stood in their path. It was a huge, questing orange serpent, but it had no eyes or mouth. It had reared up outside the cave and twitched, sensing their very presence. The trio froze in silence, hoping the exploring serpent wouldn't find them.

'Hold still,' mouthed George.

Leroy snapped. 'Keep it away from me,' he yelled. He let go of Andrea and flew for the furthest corner of the cave.

The serpent's head darted after him, almost too fast for Andrea's eyes to follow.

Leroy was screaming, and Andrea turned to go to him – because she felt that somehow, for some reason, it was up to her – but George was dragging her away, telling her, 'It's too late, there's nothing we can do for him now!'

And then Leroy wasn't screaming any longer. When Andrea looked back at him, he had vanished.

She and George had almost reached the blue circle, the open sky, and she spread her eagle's wings wide and blinked in the dazzling sunlight…and in that moment, George was snatched from her side by another orange snake.

They aren't serpents, thought Andrea. *They're more like…*

She had seen something like this before, if only she could remember.

Tentacles! she thought. *They're the tentacles of a*

monster, and they go on forever.

The sky was full of them, reaching for her, and in panic, suddenly alone, Andrea stumbled back into the safety of the cave, away from them.

But the first tentacle was waiting for her.

It struck towards her like a whip. She tried to outfly it, but the tentacle wrapped around her, pinning her wings to her sides. And then, the end of the tentacle opened its mouth, only there were no teeth, nothing at all, inside it – just a long black tunnel that pulled her in.

Andrea didn't scream. Instead, a single tear trickled from her eye. She finally remembered that the monster was once her beloved Mark.

Then, everything went black again.

30

Jonah and Sam watched the sunrise.

They stood at the deck rail of the Guardian barge, in the same spot at which Jonah had stood with his dad on a similar dawn, two mornings ago, but what felt like a lifetime.

The boat swayed on a gentle tide. Jonah knew he needed to rest, but he'd been too wired to sleep. He'd hoped the fresh air might clear his head. Sam had had the same idea. Captain Tiller was on the bridge, keeping watch for rival pirates or worse, the *Marin Avenger*.

'Where is she?' Sam asked Jonah.

He opened his palms: empty. 'I put her back inside the Metasphere. She's with the others, in their secret cave.'

'I bet she's furious with you.'

'Then she should have chosen someone else to usurp. I told her you were off-limits and I meant it.'

'Thank you, Jonah,' said Sam.

'You would've done the same for me,' said Jonah. He believed it. He felt tied to Sam, connected to her; they would look after each other.

'I can't quite believe I'm back in control of my body, of my own brain.'

'What…what was it like?' asked Jonah. 'Being usurped?'

'It was like…like being trapped in someone else's dream,' said Sam.

'A dream?' Jonah recalled his dad saying something similar.

'It was like I was only partly there most of the time. I knew what was happening but it didn't really affect me, you know? Except, there *were* some times, like when Andrea was taking prisoners or when she briefed her army to fight the Millennials and I knew they couldn't possibly win…'

Sam took a deep, calming breath. 'Those times, I just wanted to scream. I wanted to reach out and grab Andrea by her wings and shake some sense into her, but I couldn't because she was…because she was *me* and I was stuck inside.' Sam seized up, and Jonah thought she might cry. 'And I couldn't get her out. I tried, I really did, but I…I failed.'

'You didn't fail at anything,' said Jonah. 'I failed to protect you in the cave. I'm sorry.'

'It's OK,' said Sam, wiping her eyes. 'You did what you thought was right, and you never stopped.' Jonah turned away, thinking about what Granger had said about determination, and about impatience. 'And hey, look, I'm all right now, and we've got the Eastern Corner back, and Andrea and the Uploaded can't get to us here in the real world.'

'But the Uploaded won't stay hidden forever, will they? They'll hunt down other living avatars and usurp them.'

'I know how Andrea thinks,' said Sam. 'I was inside her mind even as she was inside mine. Did she tell you she was in the Navy? Andrea is a fighter, Jonah. She gave up once and, deep down, she's ashamed of that. She won't give up again.'

'Yeah,' sighed Jonah.

'She'll rebuild her city of the Reborn, somewhere else, and we can't let that happen. We can't let other people go through what I...' Sam's voice trailed off. 'I'm sorry,' she said. 'I wasn't thinking. Your dad...'

'No,' said Jonah. 'It's OK. I think it's time we talked about it. My dad stole Luke Wexler's body; he was addicted to life.'

'I know you loved having him back from the dead.'

'More than I can explain,' said Jonah. 'But I couldn't hold onto him forever. It wasn't right for him to be in Luke's body. I'm glad he plugged himself in and took the lead for the other Reborn to follow.'

'I understand, you know,' said Sam. 'From sharing Andrea's thoughts. I understand why she did what she did. I understand why your dad did what he did.'

'I was so... When I got him back, all those months ago, when I realised he'd copied himself before he died, after all... I'd just lost my mum and I was feeling so alone, and then suddenly my dad was back, and it was like a miracle.'

'But a miracle at someone else's expense,' said Sam.

'I won't send him to the Camp, Sam. But I can't bear the thought of him hiding out in that cave forever or being captured by Granger, and I wish I could find something better for him but I can't, and I just... It feels like there's no place for him anywhere any more. There's no place in the world for my dad or for anyone like him.'

Sam turned to look at the stunning sunrise, and Jonah followed her gaze.

'My mother never Uploaded,' Sam said, almost whispering.

Without turning to look at her, holding his eyes on the horizon, Jonah asked, 'What happened to your mum, Sam?'

'Angela,' said Sam. 'That was her name. I don't really... Sometimes, it's hard to remember her face. I was only five when she...when she got sick, really sick. But I remember her hair. She had red hair like mine, and when she was in chemo, it all fell out.'

'Cancer?' asked Jonah.

'A brain tumour,' said Sam. 'It came on fast, but—'

'She didn't have time to Upload?'

Sam shook her head. 'She had time. But Mum said she didn't need the Island because she'd go to Heaven. I was too young to understand. All I could grasp was that my mum was gone and, when I asked if I could visit her – like the other kids at school could visit parents and grandparents they'd lost – it always made Axel sad, and angry. I'm not sure he ever forgave her.'

'My mum was like that too,' said Jonah. 'Not religious, I mean, but she would never have Uploaded. She always said it was unnatural.'

'I used to hate the Uploaded,' said Sam. 'I'm not proud of it. I know it's not logical, but on some level I blamed them. I thought they were selfish because they wouldn't let my mother in. Like they had some club on the Island that they wouldn't let my mum join.'

'And now?'

'I still miss her, and a little part of me is jealous of the second chance you had with your dad. And you can still visit him in the Metasphere, he's not gone forever. He's not gone like my mum.' Sam sniffled and wiped her eyes. 'But I understand more now, and I think…I'm glad Mum ended her life in the way she wanted to end it. And maybe she was right and she *is* in a better place. I hope so.'

'I don't know if there is a heaven,' said Jonah, 'but I do know that if your mum is looking down at you now, she must be really proud of you.'

Sam smiled. 'Thank you. Thank you for saying that.'

She leaned in to Jonah and, hesitantly, he reached around her and rested his arm on her shoulders. He pulled Sam close. He braced himself for her to move away, but she didn't. She rested her head between his shoulder and his chest. Despite the glorious infinite colours of the dawn in front of him, Jonah's mind was distracted by the feel of Sam's warm body next to his and by the beating of his own heart, a little faster than before.

'You two!' called Axel, throwing open the deck hatch and shouting to get their attention. 'Get down here!'

Jonah loosened his arm off Sam, worried that he'd stepped over an invisible line with her father.

'Big trouble in the Metasphere,' Axel said, looking both afraid and worried. 'All hell's broken loose!'

31

Jonah could hear screaming.

Jonah, Sam, Axel and Luke hovered over a datapad monitor which had been set up on a small table below deck, wired into the barge's servers. Jonah glimpsed a virtual city, a flash of orange in the sky, then countless tentacles slithering through the sky, sucking up avatars across the Metasphere. He thumbed the datapad, scanning sections of the Metasphere as fast as he could.

'It's happening everywhere,' Jonah concluded.

Jonah scrolled to a circus, like the one that he and Sam had visited. Avatars flew along the streets in panic, diving through their exit halos, or taking shelter in the tents and behind the carnival booths.

'Granger's squid,' said Axel. 'It's everywhere.'

'It's massive,' said Sam.

A fury of orange tentacles was stabbing out of the sky. Jonah watched one tentacle grab a terrified tarantula, and the tentacle opened up and sucked in the hairy spider. Another tentacle fastened onto a blue beetle, ripping it out of the sky. Another one inhaled a fleeing flower.

The bright blue sky of the Metasphere was filled with thousands of thrashing orange tentacles. They were hundreds of metres – even kilometres – long, snaking into and out of the frame in all directions.

'My dad's in there. I have to stop this,' said Jonah.

'How?' asked Axel. 'Go online now and you'll only get yourself snatched up by one of those things, same as everyone else.'

Luke grabbed the datapad and unlocked the source code. The screen switched from cities and avatars to sequences of code.

'No,' said Luke quietly. 'He wouldn't. Jonah would be safe. Any of you would be safe. Don't you see? Don't you see what Granger's done?'

He switched the monitor back to Metasphere mode and stabbed his finger at the monitor. A tiny piglet had just tried to fly an obstacle course through the tentacles but found itself caught. This time, as the piglet avatar was whipped away, it left behind a much larger trembling humatar.

'Uploaded,' Luke realised. 'The piglet must have been Uploaded – it had usurped the humatar. So…'

'They must've reprogrammed it since the Roman massacre,' said Sam. 'The tentacles are only targeting Uploaded.'

'Sure as shootin',' said Luke.

'At this rate,' agreed Sam, 'there'll be no Uploaded left.'

'So this is Granger's final solution,' said Axel.

Jonah tapped new coordinates into the datapad.

'What are you doing?' asked Sam.

'The cave,' Jonah explained. 'Where I deposited the Reborn. I have to see if my dad's still there.'

The image on the monitor changed again. Now, it showed the inside of the huge, candlelit cave in which Jason, Andrea and the former Reborn had been hiding. Jonah swallowed down a lump in his throat.

The cave was empty.

Hovering in the entranceway, a single orange tentacle twitched from side to side, searching the shadows for more prey.

Jonah clenched his fists, frustrated. 'I sent them back there.'

'You couldn't have known,' said Sam. 'No one could have known.'

'I should have checked,' said Jonah. 'I should have checked it was safe before…'

'Maybe some of them escaped,' suggested Axel.

'Some of them *had* escaped,' said Jonah. 'To the real world. And I put them back in there. That squid is everywhere, there's no place—'

'The Camp,' groaned Axel. He had turned pale. 'What about the Camp?'

'They'll be sitting ducks,' declared Jonah, his forehead creasing in concern. The captured Uploaded would be huddled together in the Camp, easy pickings for the squid. 'I'm going in.'

* * *

Jonah flew out of his exit halo in his virtual form – and straight into an orange tentacle.

He rebounded from it, smarting. It was just as he had feared: the sky was full of the things. It was like trying to fly through thick orange spaghetti.

He swooped under one tentacle, pushed another aside. He found a gap and dropped towards the prison island below him. The last time he had been here, the island had been sunny. Now, it lay in the shadows of a hundred writhing monsters.

The Camp was in chaos. Its Uploaded inmates were helpless in their enclosures; the tentacles were swooping down and picking them off one by one. The sound of their screaming was unbearable.

The guards were fighting back, peppering the tentacles with useless virus-bullets.

Jonah touched down beside the warthog warden, who was directing the guards.

'You have to take down the fences,' Jonah yelled over the commotion. 'You have to give the Uploaded a chance to save themselves.'

'No way,' said the warthog, his tusks wobbling as he shook his head firmly. 'They'd usurp us in a second and be out of here through our exit halos. That's the only way they *can* save themselves.'

Jonah knew he was right.

'There has to be a way—' he began.

'*Look out!*' someone yelled. Jonah turned, but

before he knew it an orange tentacle had smacked into him and sent him spinning through the air.

He struggled to right himself, preparing for the next blow. But the tentacle wasn't interested in him. He had just been in its way.

It plunged through a razor wire fence as if it wasn't there. It pinned a giant slug – slower than its fellow inmates to get out of the tentacle's path – up against the far side of the enclosure, and opened up wide. Three or four guards shot bullets into the length of the tentacle. To Jonah's astonishment, it froze.

Jonah flew up to the warthog's side again. 'What are they shooting?'

'The strongest viruses we've got,' said the warthog. 'It won't slow it for more than...'

There was no need to finish the sentence. The tentacle was twitching, already throwing off its paralysis. And the slug hadn't moved, clearly having succumbed to a paralysis of its own, now quaking at the opening of its orange attacker.

Jonah acted instinctively. He threw himself at the tentacle, tried to wrestle it away from the slug. The tentacle lifted Jonah into the air, flipped him over, dashed him to the ground. It reared over him for a second as if about to strike. But then, as it had before, it disregarded him completely. It lashed out at the cowering slug again and this time no one could stop it. The slug let out a wretched squeal as it was drawn inside the tentacle.

Jonah cried out, 'Let him go!'

He launched himself at the tentacle again – too late to save the slug – and he planted his hands on it, palms down.

Some time ago, Jonah had been given a deconstruction virus by a schoolmate named Harry. The code was stored in his inventory space and he summoned it up now and willed it into the tentacle. The effect, he hoped, was that the virus would eat through its orange skin. If all the tentacles were connected, then maybe, with some luck, the others would be crippled too. He knew it was a long shot, but he had to try.

But the virus had no effect. *Of course it didn't work,* Jonah told himself crossly. *This is Granger's technology. It'll be loaded up with all the antiviral products available on the market and a few that aren't yet.*

There was nothing he could do. Nothing but watch as the tentacles sucked up the last of the trapped inmates. Even the guards had lowered their guns, bowing to the inevitable. Soon, Axel and Sam arrived, floating down to stand beside Jonah. They looked as helpless as he felt, as useless as their Guardian comrades.

With their job done, with no prey left to hunt, the tentacles withdrew. Their shadows lifted from the Camp to reveal a scene of devastation. The wire fences were gone, most of them eaten through. Outbuildings had been demolished, watchtowers toppled, and the ground churned into mud.

The sun hit the island again as the tentacles retreated. Some of the old enclosures had been emptied. In others, avatars who had been usurped were now released and were blinking in the sunlight, disoriented.

Axel was trembling with rage. 'He had no right. Granger had no right to come here to Guardian territory and take those people. We promised to protect them!'

'Are they...?' The warthog padded up behind Jonah, Sam and Axel. 'Have they been destroyed? I only ask because I had a sister who Uploaded.'

Axel shook his head. 'We don't know. We just don't know.'

'Yeah, I do,' said Jonah. 'Granger is taking them off-line.'

'Then she's as good as gone,' sobbed the warthog.

'She's intact, but imprisoned within the servers on Granger's boat,' said Jonah.

'Can you get her back?' asked the warthog.

Jonah looked up, and his eyes narrowed. He was sure there were fewer tentacles in the sky than there had been, and they were...what? Shrinking? Receding into the distance... No, *retracting!* That was what they were doing. Retracting back into the mass of the great squid that had swallowed the world's Uploaded.

'But it can't be off-line at the moment,' he realised. 'The tentacles have to… Somehow, they have to *deposit* the Uploaded they've captured in Granger's prison, which means there must be a connection open right now between the Metasphere and the prison servers.'

His feet had left the ground and he chased after the retreating tentacles. Jonah looked back to see Sam and Axel flying after him.

'What are we doing?' shouted Sam.

'We're following the tentacles,' Jonah answered over his shoulder, 'to Granger's prison.'

It was easier said than done. Once more in the midst of the tentacles, they all seemed to be moving in opposite directions. Jonah found the end of one and managed to keep it in his sights, despite its haphazard course and dizzying speed. As it whipped around in a loop, he almost crashed into Axel.

'This way,' said Sam. She pointed with her unicorn's horn. 'They're going this way.'

The three avatars flew in the direction Sam had indicated.

'What's the point of this?' asked Axel.

'If the portal is open,' said Jonah, 'the door might swing both ways.'

'Jonah, listen to yourself,' shouted Axel. 'Do you really want to get the Uploaded back?'

Jonah realised that Axel was probably thinking the

same thing as every other terrified user: finally, the curse of the Uploaded had been lifted. Finally, the Metasphere was free from the hungry dead. But Jonah didn't see it that way. Sucking up the Uploaded and taking them off-line was just as wrong as the Uploaded usurping people's avatars. And this was personal. His father was in there!

'I can't let my dad become Granger's prisoner!'

Jonah flew as fast as he could, Axel and Sam still following. Jonah recognised the vast virtual city of Grangerville below.

'We're in Millennial territory!' exclaimed Sam.

'Pilgrims in an unholy land,' whispered Axel.

The streets were near deserted. Even here, it appeared the orange tentacles had run rampant. Just a handful of avatars – living avatars, presumably – could be seen, peering cautiously out of windows or around the corners of alleyways, wondering if it was safe to come out yet.

Jonah wasn't interested in them. He wanted to find where the squid was depositing its prey; he had to find Granger's prison. Hundreds of tentacles streaked past them, emptying the sky, and Jonah could see now that they were all converging upon the same distant point, past the city and out to sea.

He continued to chase the tentacles, with the unicorn and the gryphon flanking him. They followed the end of a retracting tentacle. It was too fast for them, pulling out of their reach, but they soon found another, and another.

They flew over a sparkling ocean and finally found the source of the tentacles. The squid was massive, as big as a stadium, and it hovered above an enormous prison block.

The grey complex floated above the water: a massive concrete and steel block, with no doors or windows but with tentacles wrapped around it. Jonah thought he could hear the frightened screams of the captured Uploaded, millions of voices crying for freedom. Was his father in there?

'It's still online,' shouted Jonah. 'We have to get those Uploaded out of there before Granger takes it off—'

And suddenly it was gone.

'We're too late,' said Jonah.

The building, the whole building, had just blinked out of existence – and it had taken a massive section of the sky along with it. Now, where Granger's super-prison had been a moment ago, there was now only an eerie void.

There was nothing left except the giant squid, still hovering in place above the emptiness. It was looking down at Jonah, and he could have sworn that its eyes were mocking him.

32

Jonah started at the datapad monitor, looking at the mammoth, thousand-tentacled squid with a mix of hate and determination.

He, Sam, and Axel had flown away from the void, back to their exit halos, and logged off back into the real world of the cramped stateroom to regroup where Luke had been watching them.

'He's taken my dad,' mourned Jonah. 'He's taken them all off-line.'

'There was nothing you could have done to save him,' said Luke.

'We didn't even have a chance to try,' said Jonah.

Jonah wanted to scream. He had been so close, close enough to touch the concrete building, and now...

Now, he stared at the grey void on the screen as if there might be something in there to help him. He knew it was pointless. The void was just that: a total absence of programming code.

Within an hour, the computer servers of the Millennial-controlled Northern Corner would fill the void with fresh blue pixels. It would look like any other stretch of sky.

'We have to go after him,' said Jonah. 'We can't leave any of them in Granger's hands. He'll turn them into brain-dead ghosts, or worse. He might just delete them all.'

'But what can we do?' asked Sam.

Jonah was thinking furiously. He looked at the squid, Granger's uncontrollable weapon, and had a dangerous idea. What if *they* could control it?

'That squid is designed to capture Uploaded,' said Jonah.

'We know that much,' said Axel.

'Then why don't we use it to capture them back?'

If the prison were still online, Jonah was sure the Guardians could reprogram the squid to bust through Granger's prison the way it tore its way through the Camp. But the Uploaded were now stored off-line, on Granger's boat. Jonah had a flash of memory, of Hong Kong, of logging on locally to open the Chang Bridge for his father. He needed to log on locally again, but this time the servers weren't locked in a skyscraper, they were in the lower decks of Granger's heavily armed super-boat. The Uploaded were trapped in the *Marin Avenger*, and that meant Jonah had to go back to the enemy.

'Jo-nah,' said Sam, studying his face. 'I don't like that look in your eye.'

Jonah could tell Sam knew what he intended to do.

'What look?' asked Luke.

'The suicide mission look,' sighed Sam.

'No way!' shouted Axel. Sam's father had caught on to Jonah's intention. 'Even if we could reprogram the squid, and that's a huge *if*, those servers are off-line, on Granger's boat; you said so yourself. And we can't just attack the *Marin Avenger* on the high seas and—'

'No,' said Jonah.

'Phew,' said Axel, 'for a minute there I thought you were suggesting—'

'*We* can't attack,' interrupted Jonah, 'but a band of pirates could.'

'What?' asked Sam.

'And while Granger is fighting off a pirate attack on the water...' said Jonah, gesturing with his right hand, pretending it was a boat floating on imaginary waves. He slowly brought his left hand up to cup the underside of the boat. 'We'll sneak in underwater in Howie's submarine and extract that data.'

'You're crazy, you know that, right?' teased Axel.

'Tell me there's a sane option,' challenged Jonah, 'and I'll happily take it.'

'And if we get the Uploaded back?' asked Sam. 'What then? There are millions of them.'

Jonah knew he couldn't put them back in the mix, back in the Metasphere with the living users. But that didn't mean they had to live like prisoners, in a concentration camp. Granger had said that he intended to build a new Island, and although Jonah didn't trust his words one bit, he wondered, now that the Guardians controlled the Eastern Corner, whether they could allocate enough server space to give the Uploaded a new Island, an off-line Island. People could commune with the dead using Granger's new meta-windows between the real world and the Metasphere, but the Uploaded would be contained and not tempted by the lives of others.

Jonah explained it to Axel and Sam and, for the first time in his life, felt like a leader. Perhaps Granger was right; perhaps he did have what it takes.

'Who's going to hack the squid?' asked Sam. 'The Guardian techs are all prepping for the Northern Corner attack.'

'Lucky we've got the world's best programmer right here,' said Jonah, looking at Luke.

'Can you really reprogram that squid, hotshot?' asked Axel.

'Can a bronco buck in the buff?' laughed Luke. Jonah took that as a 'yes.'

'And I'll free up enough space on the servers,' said Sam.

'Thank you, Sam,' said Jonah. 'And I'll call the pirates.'

'But why would they help us?' asked Axel.

'Because I don't think Howie wants to be a pirate at all,' speculated Jonah. 'I think if he had a choice, a legitimate way to take care of his people, he'd take it.'

'And what would that way be?' asked Sam.

'Running the Eastern Corner for the Guardians,' announced Jonah.

'Hey, hey, hey!' protested Axel. 'I'm all for calling in the cavalry, but we fought and died for the Eastern Corner; we're not just going to hand it to a bunch of lawless—'

'Rocket scientists,' said Jonah. 'They're ex-NASA. These are techs and scientists who've turned to piracy out of desperation. If we let them profit from the Corner, they can have a whole new livelihood.'

'What are you playing at, kid?' asked Axel.

'I'm playing the long game,' said Jonah.

Matthew Granger stood on the deck of the *Marin Avenger*, watching his soldiers return from their war in disgrace.

Six black motorised dinghies skimmed across the water towards him, leaving the disastrous battle of Miami Beach behind them. One by one, they tied up alongside the *Avenger* and their bedraggled occupants climbed aboard.

The first few of them glanced at Granger, expecting he would have something to say to them. He just wanted them out of his sight. He couldn't look at them.

All Granger could think about was what these

bunglers had cost him. *I should have left them to stew in their own juices*, he thought darkly. But the pirate Howie had been right. He needed *someone*.

The Millennial soldiers continued to file past Granger, heading for their cabins below.

Of them all, only Sander's three-person platoon hesitated for a moment. The platoon leader's right leg was amputated and his stump cauterised. He leaned on Yuri and opened his mouth to speak, no doubt to offer an excuse.

Granger silenced him with nothing but a stare.

Helen couldn't bring herself to meet her leader's gaze. And so it was left to the usually aloof Yuri to look Granger straight in the eye and say, 'I am sorry, Mr Granger. We have failed you.'

Granger ignored the apology. He was unwilling to accept or forgive a failure of this magnitude.

'Where is Jonah Delacroix?' he asked. 'Did he return with you?'

'We lost him when Sander got shot,' admitted Helen. 'I don't know if he made it out of there alive.'

Granger had sincerely hoped that Jonah would join his cause; put his rash, but unending determination to work for the greater Millennial vision, to fight for a future that was worth inhabiting. The boy had likely chosen another path this time. But Jonah would come to Granger in the end, wanting a deal – with the Guardians' blessing or without it.

Granger turned to a waiting helmsman. 'Tell the captain to raise anchor,' he instructed him, 'and get us underway.'

'Yes, sir,' said the helmsman. 'Where to, sir?'

'North,' said Granger.

33

Howard O'Brien surveyed the devastation of Miami Beach.

The sand was strewn with spent cartridges and the remains of wooden barricades. Several boats had been damaged, a few gutted by fire, and there were bodies to be cremated, attackers and defenders both. There was a lot of work to do to restore a sense of normality, whatever that was.

The ransom he'd got from Granger, ten million meta-dollars, wouldn't bring back the dead but it would make life easier for those who survived. Howie stood at the centre of the mess, directing the clean-up. His surviving people worked harder than they had worked before, because they knew they owed their lives to their fallen comrades.

Howie wanted to provide for his people. He had been on the radio to some contacts already, people who could use the virtual money that Granger had paid him. People who could provide much-needed physical supplies in return. He had bought his people some time. A little time.

Even ten million meta-dollars wouldn't last long, not with food prices as high as they were and medical supplies expensive and hard to come by. But Howie wanted to build a real society, a home for their children to grow up in, not just a ramshackle hideout in the shadow of Florida's glory years.

Howie stared in surprise at a small group of people approaching him across the sand. There were eight of them altogether. Four pirates with four prisoners who were roped together, bound at the wrists. Howie rubbed his eyes, thought he must've been seeing things. He recognised the four captives, but the last thing he had expected was to meet them here again.

'Seems these so-called freedom fighters have a death wish,' said one of the pirates, a leering grin exposing gaps between his teeth.

'We caught 'em motoring up the bay in a dinghy,' said another, 'bold as brass.'

'You didn't catch us,' said a prisoner, who Howie remembered – the girl with the red hair who had been Andrea's host. He never knew her *real* name.

'No,' agreed the other kid, the smart one. The sneaky one. Jonah, he was called. 'We came here to talk to you.'

Howie raised a pierced eyebrow. 'And what if I ain't in the mood for more talk? I reckon I did all the talking I had to do on your barge.'

'Yeah,' agreed the first pirate, 'before you left us to finish what you started.'

'Which we did,' said Howie. 'We sent the

Millennials packing and made a profit into the bargain, but we paid a mighty high price for it. So, maybe what I feel like doing right now is mourning our dead, and prayin' for their immortal souls.'

The pirates lowered their eyes.

'I'm sorry for everyone you've lost,' said Jonah, 'I truly am. I know this isn't the life you wanted for your family. And I'm here to offer you a new one, an honest one.'

'Oh, yeah? How's that?'

'By running the Eastern Corner,' announced Jonah. 'Right, Axel?'

The red-headed girl's father with the intense eyes and the scraggly beard nodded, and Howie blinked in disbelief. Then he laughed. But no one was laughing with him. He narrowed his eyes. 'What is this, your idea of a joke?'

'I said the same at first,' said Axel. 'But you know what's funny, Howie? It's not even the craziest idea the kid's ever had.'

'It makes good sense,' said the other man. Howie only knew him as Jonah's father.

'The Guardians don't have the sort of organised network that the Millennials have,' added Axel. 'Our plan was to distribute the micro-servers to our supporters across the world. But most of those supporters have their hands full already.'

'Which is where you come in,' said Jonah. 'You

could run the Eastern Corner from here. Run it properly, I mean. It would be like…like the Guardians have subcontracted its management to you.'

'You recognised the micro-servers when you saw them,' said the girl. 'You're pretty comfortable around technology.'

'Something like that,' Howie muttered. 'We know a thing or two about a thing or two.'

'And you and your community would take a cut from every meta-transaction handled by your servers,' explained Jonah.

'A fair cut,' said Axel. 'Set by the Guardians.'

'But enough,' said Jonah. 'Enough to build something real here. Enough to stop being pirates.'

It sounded too good to be true.

'OK, so what's the catch?' asked Howie. He saw the nervous looks that passed between the four Guardians, and he knew he had been right. 'I know you ain't doing this just out of the goodness of your hearts – so, what do you want from us?'

'There *is* something,' said Jonah. 'We need you to be pirates just one last time.'

Granger hated being woken in the middle of the night – and especially when it was for bad news. These days, it always seemed to be bad news…

'What the hell do those bandits think they're playing at now?' he bellowed as he marched out of his stateroom on his cyber-kinetic legs, pulling on his grey tracksuit.

'We've tried to raise them on the radio,' Vierra explained, scurrying to keep ahead of him. 'But they're approaching fast, too fast to be friendly.'

'How many?' asked Granger. 'How many boats are there?'

'Eight, sir,' she said. 'Just eight but they're smaller and faster than we are. They're gaining on us. The captain thought you ought to be informed.'

Granger climbed up onto the *Marin Avenger*'s broad deck. He strode to the stern, where a small group of Millennials had gathered. They parted to allow him through.

The pursuing boats were already closer than he had anticipated.

There were eight of them, as Granger had been told: a motley assortment of battle-worn vessels, with tattered pirate flags flying proudly in the moonlight.

'It doesn't make sense,' Granger muttered to himself. 'I knew O'Brien was a greedy man. I didn't think he was this stupid.'

Sander was beside him, steadying himself on a crutch, holding up a pair of binoculars. 'I've been taking a closer look at those boats, sir, and—'

Granger snatched the binoculars from him and raised them to his own eyes. Sander carried on speaking anyway, confirming what Granger could now see for himself.

'As far as I can tell, they have a fraction of our firepower.'

But enough to do us some damage, thought Granger, though he didn't say it out loud.

'Jonah Delacroix,' said Granger.

'Beg your pardon, sir?'

'He's behind this, I know it. Howard O'Brien *isn't* stupid. He's had ten million meta-dollars of my money today. He has no reason to carry out a suicidal stunt like this in the slim hope of getting more. No reason unless...'

'You think the Guardians got to him?' asked Sander.

'What could they have possibly offered him?' mused Granger. He pivoted on his heel and marched back the way he had come. He raised his voice so that every Millennial on the deck would hear him.

'Battle stations!' instructed Granger. 'As soon as those boats are within weapons range, you're to fire at will. Don't let me down again. Thanks to you, the Howard O'Briens of this world think we are a soft target. Well, this is your chance to show them – and me – otherwise. I want all eight of those boats resting at the bottom of the sea by the time I finish my first cup of coffee.'

* * *

Jonah stood beside Sam on the bow of the largest boat next to Howie, speeding towards the *Marin Avenger*. The pirate boats had been modified for fast attack. The plan was simple: the pirate boats would distract Granger while Howie would take Sam and Jonah in the mini-sub, and latch onto the hull of the *Avenger*. Once attached, Jonah and Sam would slip in and log into Granger's servers – the ones that held the Uploaded. Luke had successfully hacked the squid virus and Jonah would direct it to pull out all of the incarcerated Uploaded and transfer them back to the ring-fenced servers housed on the Guardians' barge.

A bright flash popped on the *Avenger*, followed by a thunderclap.

'Brace yourself!' called Howie.

It was a straightforward plan, but it wasn't without risk. The pirates were putting themselves in harm's way on the high seas.

Something screeched low over their heads. Jonah followed the rocket soaring overhead, narrowly missing them. An explosion behind them lit up the night sky for an instant. Jonah squinted his eyes as he was buffeted by hot air. He stumbled blindly into the deck rail as the pirate boat lurched crazily. He heard the distant *crumps* of two more missiles being fired.

Fortunately, these two were a lot further off-target than the first had been. One of them fell short and disappeared beneath the waves. The other went far wide, creating a shooting star in the eastern sky.

Unlike Jonah, Howie had kept his footing throughout the turbulence. He barked instructions to his small armada through a loudhailer: 'Fan out and keep moving. Don't give them an easy target. And don't return fire yet. Not until we're closer in. Let Granger's people waste their ammo if they—'

Howie's voice was cut off. The *Marin Avenger* had launched a fourth and fifth missile, and once again the pirate boats were rocked by nearby explosions.

'To the sub,' ordered Howie to Jonah and Sam, his voice filled with urgency.

He led Jonah and Sam to the aft of the boat. The night sky was filled with crackling lights and smoke and chaos, and Jonah spotted that one of the other pirate boats had actually caught fire. Crew members were scurrying around its deck with fire extinguishers, and suddenly Jonah felt in his gut what he'd known in his head but hadn't wanted to acknowledge: people were going to get killed out here.

'Drop back,' Howie ordered one of his crew. 'Let the other boats draw the enemy's fire until I tell you to—'

'*Incoming!*' someone yelled, and suddenly there was a tremendous blast of noise and heat. Jonah pushed Sam down instinctively and dived on top of her.

'Ow!' she screamed. Jonah clumsily raised himself on his elbows, catching himself looking into her green eyes as he steadied himself. 'But thanks.'

She leapt to her feet, and dragged Jonah up with her. They chased after Howie, Jonah's ears ringing, numbed by the explosion – the closest one yet. All around, people were running, yelling. It took a moment for their words to penetrate his deadened ears: '*Men overboard!*'

Jonah saw a life ring hanging nearby. He grabbed it and ran to the side of the deck. He spotted Aldrin struggling to tread the choppy water and he tossed the ring to him.

He only just made the throw. The boat was still ploughing forwards, away from its lost crew members. Jonah made out six, no, seven more bodies in the water and at least four more life rings drifting between them.

Jonah called for Howie, who was rushing towards two pirates struggling with a rocket launcher, 'We have to turn back for them!' But Howie was focused on the rocket system. The tripod on which it had been mounted, ready for use, had collapsed. One pirate hefted the weapon while the other loaded a long, arrow-shaped rocket – bigger than the Millennials' rockets – into the muzzle.

Howie took over from them, pulling rank. He crouched on one knee with the launcher on his shoulder. The smoke around the pirate boats cleared for a second, and Jonah's heart leapt into his throat at the sight of the *Marin Avenger*, so much closer ahead than it had been before.

When Howie fired the rocket, Jonah watched with bated breath as its payload streaked away into the night. The rocket hit the hull of Granger's boat and detonated. Jonah knew that the key was to damage and distract the *Avenger*, not to sink it.

Scaling the aft railing, Howie beckoned Jonah and Sam after him. They climbed down the ladder dangling behind the boat, down to the waiting submarine.

Howie opened the clear canopy and waved Jonah and Sam in after him. Jonah ushered Sam in first, lifting himself down and into the small space behind her.

The cockpit only had two seats – Howie at the controls and Sam in the navigator's chair – leaving Jonah to close the hatch above him and lock it tight. With the cockpit occupied, Jonah had to squeeze himself into a narrow storage area behind Sam's seat, lying flat on his stomach. When the top hatch was sealed, Howie activated the engines.

Jonah heard the sucking sound of airtight seals engaging, and found himself wondering how much air there could possibly be in this cramped compartment. He felt claustrophobic, but tried to quash the rising panic in his gut. There was no going back.

'Our range is limited,' explained Howie. 'That's why we had to get up so close to our target before we launched it.'

The sound of the explosions were muffled in here. Jonah realised that they had also grown more distant. It seemed the other pirate boats had succeeded in distracting the Millennial guns from this one, the important one. Which meant, of course, that Axel and the other pirates were in more danger than ever.

The submarine dived down below the underbelly of Howie's boat, keeping them safe. For now.

'The sonar's got a good lock on the *Marin Avenger*,' the pirate leader continued, looking at his instrument panels. 'So, assuming this old thing performs to the specifications I drew up for it...'

'*You* drew up?' asked Sam.

'Toldja he wasn't just a pirate,' said Jonah.

'Jonesy's right. I designed and built this sub myself, with a little help from some of the others, out of old rocket parts – you don't have to sound quite so surprised to hear it! I told you right from the off what I did for a living.'

'You mean you really were –' said Sam – 'you *are*...a rocket scientist?'

'Like most of the others, I worked for NASA,' confirmed Howie, 'until the whole thing was shut down. Heck, we were about to launch us our own satellite to track ships on the open ocean. But if this plan works, if we can really run the Eastern Corner, then we'll gladly put our pirate days behind us.'

Howie pushed on his control stick and the submarine surged forwards. They were on their way to the *Avenger*.

Jonah just hoped the plan would work, for everyone.

34

Jonah couldn't believe he was underneath Granger's boat.

If he hadn't been trying to save the Uploaded, they could have ripped a hole big enough in the hull to sink the *Marin Avenger* once and for all. But that's not what Jonah came for.

'Locking on now,' said Howie. 'Hold onto—'

Before he could finish speaking, the sub was buffeted by the blast-wave from an explosion above water.

It couldn't have happened at a worse moment. The hull of Granger's ship, the part of it that was below the surface, was a great dark shape off their port side. Howie had been manoeuvring towards it, slowly, carefully. Now, the sub's controls flew out of his hands and they veered straight into their target.

Jonah's winced at the screech of metal against metal, and he feared that their smaller vessel might be torn right open. Jonah cursed his previous thoughts about sinking the vessel. It was his submarine that might be lost at sea.

But Howie deftly regained control of his sub and steered them sharply out of danger. A moment later, they were slowly edging towards the *Marin Avenger*'s hull again, Sam and Jonah both holding their breath.

This time there were no surprises and Howie's hand stayed sure and steady. 'Matching speed,' he muttered, 'and engaging magnetic clamps...*now*!'

Jonah braced himself as the sub gave a brief, violent shudder, reminiscent of the rough – but safe – first landing he'd piloted in the outback of Australia. Howie cut the propeller, gave the instruments one final check, sat back in his seat and let out the breath that he had been holding all this time.

'Is that it?' asked Jonah. 'Are we attached?'

'The seal should be watertight. It's your turn now, Jonesy.'

Jonah's left arm was pressed up against the locking wheel of a hatch that had been welded into the side of the craft. He turned the wheel and, tentatively – not to mention awkwardly in such cramped confines – he pulled open the small circular door.

If the rocket scientist's maths skills had deteriorated in his years of piracy, Jonah would be flooded with sea water. Fortunately, Howie's attachment was perfect. Jonah found the opening he had created blocked by a dark red expanse of metal: the hull of the *Avenger*.

'My turn first,' said Sam, grabbing her drill-shaped laser cutter. Sam had spent half her life breaking into dangerous situations, using all manner of tools. To her, Jonah figured, this was just another breaking and entering job. The difference was, of course, they were six metres below sea level.

'You're sure there's no one directly on the other side?' asked Jonah, gathering extra cord to give Sam more manoeuvrability.

'Now you ask?' laughed Sam as she placed the drill's tip against the *Marin Avenger*'s hull.

'The sonar says it's vacant on the other side,' Howie explained.

'I guess we'll soon find out,' said Sam expectantly, lighting up the laser.

The end of the cutter glowed red, and its powerful beam ate through the metal hull. Once Sam had cut a circle large enough for her and Jonah to climb through, Jonah tried to pull the slab of metal away, but it fell inwards, into the hull of the *Avenger*. He winced as it landed on the other side of the hole with a resounding clang. They looked at each other silently, waiting an anxious thirty seconds, but no one came to investigate the noise.

Jonah stepped through first, scared but determined. He emerged into a cabin on board the *Marin Avenger*. The room appeared to be in use: clothes were strewn across a chair and a half-eaten Pro-Meal pouch was congealing on the table. Jonah was relieved that the cabin was empty – at least for now.

Jonah hurried to the door and listened at it. He couldn't hear anything. He eased the door open and peered around the edge. Jonah recognised the corridor and fortunately it was empty too.

He turned to Sam, who was just climbing through the hole behind him.

'I think we're close to the control room,' whispered Jonah. 'And I don't see any Millennials.'

'They must all be up top,' said Sam, 'fighting off Howie's pirates.'

A muffled explosion, causing the floor to give a lurch beneath their feet, reminded them that they were still in the middle of a war. Howie had deemed it 'unlikely' that Granger's tanker could be sunk by the pirates' guns, but there was always that chance. 'And trust me on this,' he had told them, reminding Jonah of Sam's earlier warning, 'there's no such thing as *friendly* fire.'

They crept out of the empty cabin and scurried to the nearest corner. Sam checked that the way was clear, then signalled to Jonah to follow her round. She had drawn her pistol and looked ready to use it.

They passed more cabin doors and reached a T-junction. Jonah saw a door marked 'Galley', and grinned. He had been this way before with Granger and he took comfort in the familiarity.

Sam was waiting for directions. Jonah pointed down the left arm of the 'T'. As he did so, the ceiling lights flickered as the boat was rocked by another missile.

The two Guardians exchanged a nervous glance.

A second later, they abandoned all pretence of stealth and pelted down the long corridor side by side.

They stood outside the server-room door.

Sam mouthed to Jonah, '*Are you ready?*'

Jonah nodded.

He closed his hand around the doorknob, turning it slowly. Once he could feel that the latch was disengaged, he nodded to Sam again. She drew back her right foot.

Jonah let go of the door at the precise instant that Sam's boot struck it.

The door flew open and Sam leapt through it. Jonah glimpsed white walls, a bank of computer servers and a young man in black combat fatigues, who spun around to face the unexpected intruders.

Sam fired her pistol twice. The young man's face froze in a grimace. He clutched his hands to his stomach and fell off his chair. But even though Sam had stopped firing, Jonah could still hear gunshots, coming from a near corner of the room that he couldn't see. There was someone else in there!

Sam ducked back into the doorway and almost collided with Jonah. She fired three times around the doorframe, and the answering shots from inside the room ceased.

Sam waited for a second to be sure, then went back into the control room.

Jonah followed her, wincing at the young Millennial man lying in a pool of his own blood. An older woman in a white lab coat was slumped in the corner. Both were dead. Sam had killed them both. Jonah wondered if Sam could've spared their lives. But she didn't work that way. Unlike Jonah, she shot to kill.

She had no choice, he convinced himself. *It was them or us, and we couldn't let them stop us.* He wondered if Matthew Granger ever said the same thing to himself.

'I'll watch the door,' offered Sam. 'You get on with it.'

Jonah nodded. He hurried across the room. He wasn't sure which of the many servers was the right one. He had to close his eyes and remember…

He pictured a Japanese man strapped into a black chair. He pictured Granger, shooting an orange pellet into the man's chest. And then:

Yuri picking up an orange sphere and…

That one! Yuri had squished the sphere into the DI port of *that* server.

Jonah checked the indicator lights near the top of the server tower. It was active, all right, but showing no Metasphere connection. It had to be the one. It had to be this server that housed Granger's off-line prison.

Feverishly, he dug two objects out of his pockets. The first was one of Mr Chang's new, super-efficient micro-servers, which he'd taken from Captain Tiller's barge. The second was a connecting cable. Jonah plugged the micro-server into Granger's bigger server and watched as the indicator lights on both flickered.

Now all he had to do was wait.

The micro-server contained a single virus: the reprogrammed Extractor squid. Now that Jonah had connected it to the off-line prison, it would be doing exactly what it had been created to do. It would be sending out tentacles, locating all of the Uploaded and vacuuming them up.

He felt a pang of guilt. *They must be terrified*, he thought, *facing that monster again, not knowing what it wants with them this time.*

A couple of minutes passed before Sam asked impatiently, 'How much longer?'

'I don't know,' answered Jonah, looking at the indicator lights on both servers. There were millions of Uploaded to suck out of the prison. Jonah didn't want to leave even one behind, not just because the unlucky last one could be his father, but because he wanted to live up to his moniker, he wanted to be the Uploaded's saviour once again. He felt he owed them that.

'Anyone coming?' whispered Jonah. The boat heaved again, and Sam shook her head, keeping her eyes and pistol trained on the corridor outside.

Jonah wanted to peek inside, to make sure the squid was working. He found the dead man's datapad on a desk and plugged it into the server. On screen, he saw the giant squid hovering over the prison. Because the prison was stored on the local servers, its firewalls weren't active like they were in the Metasphere. The squid's thousands of tentacles sprawled out all across the unprotected complex, sucking up the Uploaded.

'It's working,' he said with relief. Finally, after what felt like an eternity, the squid retracted the last of its tentacles and hovered about the prison.

'That's it,' said Jonah, unplugging the box. 'That's all of them.' He tried not to feel too elated too soon. But they'd done it!

'Good,' said Sam. 'Then let's get out of here, back to Howie and the sub. I haven't heard any explosions for a while, and so I think…I think the pirates must have been forced to break off their attack, which means—'

'Which means we don't have a distraction any longer.'

Jonah rushed to catch up with Sam, racing down the empty corridor to be reunited with Howie and the sub.

35

Granger watched from the bridge as the pirate boats, battered and beaten, turned tail and fled.

'We did it, sir,' crowed the now one-legged Sander, limping onto the bridge on crutches. 'We fought them off.'

'Keep firing after them,' insisted Granger, clenching his fists. 'Keep firing!'

His people needed no encouragement. Emboldened by their enemies' retreat, they were reloading and discharging rocket launchers as quickly as they could.

Seconds later, he was rewarded by an orange blossom of fire erupting from the ocean's surface. He grinned at the direct hit. One of the pirate boats had burst into flaming wreckage. There had been no time for the people on board to escape.

'Cease fire,' Granger commanded.

'But, sir,' protested Sander. 'We can finish them off now.'

'Let them live, let them retreat,' Granger crowed. 'Let them go back to their hovels and calculate the price of their arrogance.'

Granger wanted the pirates to spread the word that they'd lost. They had attacked the *Marin Avenger* and been defeated. It would serve as a warning to others.

'Mr Granger!' called Helen, bursting onto the bridge. 'We have a problem, sir…'

He stopped in his tracks, took a deep breath and steeled himself for bad news. Something in Helen's eyes told Granger this was serious.

'We've checked the instruments,' she explained. 'And there's no doubt. We don't know how it happened, maybe one of the pirates had a torpedo, but…but we're taking on water, fast.'

Granger just stared, trapped in a nightmare.

A part of his brain insisted that this couldn't be happening, and wanted him to wake up. Another part had noticed that his boat was sailing lower in the water than it ought to have been and that the deck was beginning to list.

'We're sinking?' asked Granger.

Jonah clutched the micro-server to his chest. They had succeeded in their mission, the Uploaded were safe, but there was no celebration aboard the submarine. Howie had disengaged the craft from Granger's boat and it was slicing through the water back the way it had come.

Sam broke the silence, allowing herself a little smile of satisfaction: 'That big round hole we left in Granger's hull should give him something to think about.'

But they didn't yet know the full cost of their victory.

'If the pirate boats are retreating…' ventured Jonah.

Howie nodded. 'They're faster than we are. We'll never catch them up.'

'You said the sub only had a short range. Can we…?'

Howie confirmed Jonah's fears. 'The fuel tank will run dry before we can make it back to land. A long time before. We'll run out of air too.'

'What do we do?'

'To start with,' said Howie, 'we get as far away from Granger as we can with the fuel we have. After that, we won't have much choice. We'll have to surface.'

'But the sub will float, right?' said Sam.

'She'll float,' promised Howie. 'And we can throw back the hatch, so at least we'll be able to breathe.'

'But we'll be stranded,' said Jonah. 'Adrift on the ocean.'

'My people will come back for us,' said Howie.

'I hope you're right,' muttered Sam, clearly deflated.

'They will,' insisted Jonah. 'And Axel will come back. He'll search for as long as it takes to get you back.' But Jonah knew what Sam was thinking. What if Axel was aboard one of the pirate vessels that got hit?

Howie must've been thinking it too. 'He'll be good as gold,' he said. 'Yer old man's a survivor, like me.'

A hush returned to the submarine after that. None of them acknowledged what all three of them were thinking: that there must have been many casualties from the battle, on both sides; that some pirate boats might not have retreated but in fact have been destroyed; that they might have few allies left alive to worry about their fate.

They drifted for six long hours. Once they'd run short of fuel, Howie had surfaced the sub and Jonah threw open the hatch. The mini-sub had a natural buoyancy, and Sam and Jonah climbed on top of the blue hull.

As they sat together, Jonah noticed that the ocean was surprisingly calm, reflecting the moonlight and occasionally the stars above. The only sound was the gentle lapping of water against the sides of the hull of the sub.

Howie had dozed off in his seat. Jonah admired his ability to do that, but he was too tense to sleep. He couldn't stop thinking about when they would be rescued and by whom.

They'd used up their drinking water hours ago and Jonah was thirsty. He bristled at the injustice of being surrounded by water, none of which they could drink.

'I remember the last time I felt this thirsty,' he said,

thinking back to when he and Sam were imprisoned by the Lakers in Santa Monica.

'Me too,' said Sam. 'Feels like a long time ago.'

'But it wasn't,' realised Jonah. 'Just part of the same endless war. Do you think it'll ever change?'

'I don't know,' admitted Sam.

'We attack Granger, he retaliates. He strikes back, we strike back. He escalates it, we escalate it. Where will it end?'

'With him dead,' said Sam.

'Maybe, but I wish it could end without anyone dying,' said Jonah. 'And if we kill Granger, I bet there'll be another one just like him to take his place; someone with an idea of how things should run according to their way of thinking, and *only* their way of thinking.'

'And that means people like us will always have to fight for freedom,' said Sam. 'As long as there are people like Matthew Granger who are willing to kill to be in control.'

'I just wish there was another way,' sighed Jonah.

'You can't wish for that, Jonah,' Sam whispered. 'You have to fight for it.'

When Jonah heard the distant sound of an engine, he wasn't sure if it was real. Not until he saw lights on the horizon. 'There's a boat coming!' Jonah shouted down to Howie as he felt his eyes well up in relief.

Howie murmured and gruffly chided Jonah for interrupting a dream before finally asking, 'On what heading?'

Sam checked the stars and declared, 'North by north-west.'

'Miami Beach!' said Jonah with relief.

'Let's hope it's one of ours,' Howie said, climbing up onto the hull with a distress flare. Howie explained that the flare was non-pyrotechnic. It emitted a fan-shaped green laser beam, which he shone at the distant boat.

'It's working,' said Sam. 'Those lights are definitely getting closer.' Indeed, a few minutes after that, they could make out the shape of the approaching boat quite clearly and even see some figures on its deck.

Jonah heard the sound of Axel's voice on the night breeze. He had never been happier to hear Sam's dad shouting. Howie dropped the distress flare and waved.

'Dad!' called Sam. 'You found us!'

It was one of the smaller pirate boats that they sailed. Grimy hands reached down and hauled Jonah and Sam aboard. Two of those hands belonged to Axel. He pulled Sam into a long embrace. Jonah thought back to his father, and felt saddened that he'd never have a real hug from his dad ever again.

'We've been looking for you all night,' Axel said. 'But I wasn't going to give up.'

'Toldja,' said Jonah. Sam looked at him and smiled, clearly relieved.

'Did you get them?' Axel asked. 'Are they safe?'

Jonah showed him the micro-server with the Uploaded stored on it. 'Yeah, we did. They are.'

'I don't know if that means it was worth it, but I'm glad they're not in Granger's hands any more.'

'What…what happened topside?' asked Jonah, tentatively. 'Did everyone…?'

'We lost two ships,' said Axel. 'I'm sorry, Howie. One of them sunk, the other blown apart. Twenty-seven of your crew unaccounted for.'

The pirate leader's expression betrayed nothing of what he was feeling. His silence, however, said plenty.

'Irene?' asked Howie. 'And Aldrin?'

'She's fine, and we fished Aldrin and six others out of the ocean,' said Axel.

The boat's pirate crew were busy hoisting the sub on board. In the absence of the rigging that Howie's boat had, they were forced to improvise with ropes and pulleys. They performed their task in subdued silence.

Jonah knew he had been lucky. Everyone he cared about, everyone whose name he knew, had come through the battle with Granger's boat unscathed. It was different for Howie. He'd lost friends, and his friends were like family.

Jonah's plan had worked. The Guardians had got what they wanted, once again. But at what cost?

36

Jonah woke on the bow of the beached pirate ship.

He'd been so completely exhausted he'd curled up and fallen asleep on the return journey to Miami. It was the most sleep he'd had in days. Sam was still breathing heavily beside him, and he wanted to let her rest, but as soon as he stirred, she rose.

'We're back,' said Jonah, still clutching the micro-server that housed the Uploaded. He'd slept with it, surrounded it, protected it.

It was then that he noticed a line of people – pirates and their families – snaking along the sand. It took him a moment to work out what they were doing. He got it: they were taking the Eastern Corner. They were transferring the micro-servers from the Guardians' barge to a larger boat of their own.

Of course, the servers were still active and had to remain connected up, which complicated the pirates' task. Jonah was pleased to see they were taking it slowly, carefully. Howie was there, giving orders, and Jonah spotted Irene and Aldrin on another boat, coordinating the new server array. Jonah jumped down from his rescue boat and went to join them, Sam not far behind.

Howie saw them coming. 'Well, you two, look who's finally dragged themselves up,' he boomed cheerfully. 'Come to give us a hand, eh, Jonesy, now that most of the hard work has been done? You too, Sam.'

'Um, yeah, of course,' said Jonah, still groggy, 'if you like. And I wanted to say thank you. For helping us last night. We couldn't have… I mean, if it hadn't been for you and your people's sacrifice…'

'They led a pirate's life,' said Howie. 'And they died doing something that will help our entire community. Those Uploaded may have taken over our heads, our bodies, but all of us who were usurped came to understand what made them tick. They became a part of us. So you build them that Island, you keep them happy and safe…'

'We will,' said Jonah.

'…and sequestered,' added Howie.

'Let's link this server with some of the spare servers,' Sam suggested.

'The off-line ones, right?' asked Howie.

Jonah nodded. 'We can give them some more room in there, and I'd really like to talk to my dad.' He smiled at the thought, but felt a pang of guilt, knowing that Sam could never commune with her mother, and that Howie's people had lost friends and family, forever.

* * *

In an empty cabin within the beached Guardian barge, Luke helped Jonah, Sam and Axel link the micro-server with five others, giving the Uploaded a massive amount of processing power and a near-infinite space to move about.

'This'll give 'em a Texas-sized space to roam,' Luke said.

'Hopefully that's enough,' said Axel, 'to give them peace.'

Jonah hoped the Uploaded would be comfortable in their new servers. Looking at the five new micro-servers he was overwhelmed by a sense of responsibility. In front of him, six little grey boxes housed most of the world's recent dead.

So when Jonah tethered his datapad to peer inside, and couldn't see any of them, he panicked. There was only one inhabitant inside the closed system: the squid.

It had swallowed up all of the Uploaded and it wasn't releasing them.

'That's not what I programmed it to do,' said Luke.

'I don't understand,' panted Jonah. 'They should all be out, free.'

'It must be a glitch,' said Sam, her eyes desperately pleading with Luke to intervene. Luke tried to hack the virus, but nothing he did made the squid budge. It was holding onto the Uploaded, ignoring his override commands and impervious to his hack.

'What happened?' said Jonah. 'Why isn't it releasing them?'

He was looking at the orange squid. It was floating against a pure white background and appeared to be glaring right out of the screen at Jonah, taunting him.

'It doesn't make any sense,' said Sam. 'Luke, you reprogrammed it to give us total control.'

'Sure did,' said Luke. 'But it's like this here virus has a mind of its own. A stubborn one.'

'Of course. It's *alive*,' said Jonah. 'Part of it is.'

'No, it's a virus,' corrected Axel.

'A virus fused to an Uploaded avatar,' Jonah said. 'I don't know why I didn't see it until now, but that squid does have a mind of its own.' Jonah groaned, realising that his plan had backfired. 'I thought I was saving the Uploaded, but instead I've trapped them inside the belly of that beast!'

His eyes scanned the bare room until they found a small pile of DI adaptor packs. He snatched one up and tore it open. 'They must be terrified,' he said as he attached the adaptor to a trailing Ethernet wire.

'You aren't going in there?' said Sam.

'I have to,' insisted Jonah. 'I made a promise.'

He sat against the wall and felt for the socket in his back. He pushed the Direct Interface adaptor into it, making sure it clicked twice. Jonah set his Point of Origin coordinates to the local server and prepared to face the squid.

* * *

Jonah rode out the usual wave of nausea and disorientation.

He opened the eyes of his humatar to find himself in a massive white space, a room which could have been the size of a continent, stretching as far as Jonah could see. It should have contained the newly freed Uploaded, but instead it was just Jonah dwarfed by the orange squid.

The squid hovered in the centre of the room. Jonah caught his breath. When he had looked at the squid on the monitor, he'd had nothing to measure it against. He hadn't realised that, since the last time he had seen it, the squid had grown exponentially.

The orange virus towered over him and, looking up into its threatening, twitching eyes, Jonah shivered at the magnitude of the task that lay ahead of him. If he couldn't get the Uploaded out from the outside, what about from the inside? What if he could get the squid to suck him in? Once he was inside, he might be able to lead the Uploaded out.

'Sam!' called Jonah. A meta-window opened, and Jonah looked up to see Sam watching him in the closed system. 'That squid once went on the rampage, taking live avatars as well as Uploaded. We figured its processing power was over-stoked, remember?'

Sam shook her head. 'I don't like where you're going with this.'

'If you send more power to the virus, it'll take me in.'

'It's worth a go, Jonah,' said Luke, peering through the meta-window. 'If you really want to get into that beast, that is.'

Axel pushed Luke and Sam aside, pressing his face against the window so that Jonah could only see one of his eyes and his nose. 'Don't do it, Jonah! Log off at once and stop trying to be their saviour!'

'He'd do it for me,' Jonah said. 'And he'd do it for you.' Now that his father was immortal, digitally immortal, he wasn't going to let Jason waste away inside that thing for eternity. He couldn't abandon his dad to that fate.

'We're increasing power now,' said Sam, not doubting Jonah for a second.

The squid twitched and convulsed. Its eyes bulged and its tentacles flailed uncontrollably. Jonah held his ground, whispering to the squid, taunting it.

'I'm the only one in here. Come and get me.'

In response, an orange tentacle darted from the white sky and sucked Jonah into darkness.

37

And then there was light; millions of pinpricks of light against a vast darkness.

They looked like fireflies, dancing in front of Jonah's eyes, or stars, moving against the heavens.

Jonah was floating, and he couldn't find an up or a down. There was no floor, no ceiling, and seemingly no end to the infinite space all around him.

'Dad!' he cried. 'Where are you, Dad?'

Welcome, Jonah Delacroix. We are glad you are here.

Jonah couldn't tell where this echoing voice was coming from. It sounded like it was all around him. He couldn't tell if it was male or female, young or old, but he felt that some part of the voice was familiar, though he couldn't place it.

We have been waiting for you.

One of the points of light floated close to Jonah, hovered in the air and turned red. Jonah floated backwards and the tiny red light grew into his father's avatar, the red dragon.

Jason materialised from the light and spoke: 'It's good to see you, son.'

Jonah was confused; he didn't understand what was happening, but he was relieved to see his father, even in digital form. Jonah threw his arms around the dragon's hulking torso, and Jason enveloped his son in his scaly wings.

'I thought I'd lost you forever,' sobbed Jonah. 'I – I'm so sorry that you left the real world.'

'You were right, Jonah,' said the dragon, releasing from the embrace and bending his neck down to be eye-to-eye with his humatar son. 'I overstayed my welcome in the real world. Please apologise to Luke for me. He was a good host, and, in life, I'd like to think a good friend.'

'But you're trapped in here, inside this monster.'

'No, Jonah. I'm not trapped. I could leave if I wanted to. But why would I?'

'I…I don't understand.'

'Jonah, when you sent Mark to pull us from Granger's prison, something extraordinary happened. We all became connected. All of the Uploaded, all of us, are now…*one*. We share each other's thoughts and dreams. I can't explain it, Jonah, but it's beautiful; it's a higher form of consciousness.'

We are one. We are all together now. Open your mind and let us show you.

Jonah now understood what the voice was. It wasn't just one voice. It was Andrea, it was George, it was Leroy, it was his nan, it was D'Iferno, it was Amaza, it was the voices of all the Uploaded.

Every single one.

The voice of millions, all speaking as one. The voice was soft, reassuring, and what's more it wasn't coming from the darkness around Jonah or even from the dancing lights.

The voice was speaking inside his head.

Jonah turned to his father, confused and unsettled. 'Dad, I don't understand.'

But even as he said the words, Jonah knew they weren't true.

He had felt something like this before. For a short time a few months ago, Jonah's brain had stored two avatars: his father's and his own. He'd had two sets of memories and at first the foreign set had overwhelmed him. He had to learn how to hold them both, how to access his dad's memories while retaining his own sense of self. This was like that, only on a bigger scale. A much, much bigger scale.

Jonah could sense the thoughts of every one of the Uploaded, like a river crashing into the dam of his fragile mind. He had instinctively blocked them out to protect himself, and his sanity, which was what left him feeling so confused.

He looked at his dad now, however, and the dragon gave him an encouraging nod. Reassured, Jonah lifted the dam, just a little, and he let the Uploaded trickle in.

And Jonah swam on the surface of their memories. It was like every droplet of water in the river was a captured moment, released as it burst against Jonah's face. He felt the joy of seeing a new baby, the frustration of fighting a losing a battle against disease, the sadness of losing a parent, a child, and the elation of first love. A million lives lived, rushing through Jonah's head. The images were flashes, emotional memories, and Jonah started to sort through them. He latched onto the familiar. He found his grandmother's memories, saw his father as a baby, as a child, and then growing into a man. He watched his mother and father on their wedding day as they beamed at one another, full of love, hope and potential. He saw the Uploading room where Jason and Miriam comforted Jonah's nan, and said their final goodbyes while holding a very young Jonah in their arms. And then she was gone, replaced by another set of memories.

Jonah felt the fear of growing up in a violent housing project in Washington, D.C. It was Andrea's life. He saw her brother gunned down because he was wearing the wrong shoes. He watched helplessly as her mother wasted away from drink and drugs, and felt the pride and purpose of Andrea's accomplishments in the Navy. He felt her wariness towards a handsome man called Mark, and her eventual friendship, and love, as they pledged to spend their lives together. He relived the helicopter crash, her time in recovery, knowing she'd never live unassisted again, and felt Mark's hand on hers as they Uploaded together.

He felt George's life flow through his brain, the dedicated life of a doctor and a husband. He loved his Margaret with all of his being, relived the horror of watching her taken from him by the squid. And then Jonah felt Margaret's life, a woman in love, now spending eternity with her husband.

Jonah felt the lives pass through him, imprinting themselves on his heart. Even though they were dead, these were real people with real lives. They were digital now, just ones and zeroes, but those ones and zeroes added up to whole lives. And the overwhelming feeling was love.

Jonah could feel it in each of them, all of them, at once and together. Despite all of the hardships, sadness, and turmoil, it was love that filled his heart.

He didn't want to stop, and he knew he could spend his entire life inside, reliving the lives of others. But he had a life to live, on the outside. A life he wasn't done with. He gently pushed the images away; he sealed the dam in his mind as gently as he could.

As the memories faded away, they left an indelible imprint on his mind, and on his heart. Jonah heard himself letting out a blissful sigh as he opened his eyes.

Jason was still beside him, holding him with one wing. 'You understand, son, don't you?'

'Yes,' said Jonah. 'Yeah, I do. The Uploaded have become... Somehow, they're a part of one another.

They still have their own identities, but they're also...
I don't know how to describe it. They've become
a...a *whole*. And they...'

'We,' corrected Jason. '*We* don't want to leave.
We're happy in here. Everyone connected to everyone.'

'A digital Heaven,' Jonah realised.

Jason smiled.

'And you want to stay too?' Jonah had to ask the
question.

He felt his dad tensing. He didn't have to look at
his expression to know he had guessed right.

'We don't hunger for life any longer,' said Jason
quietly. 'You must have felt that for yourself. We've
found something great, a higher form of collective
consciousness. And I belong here, Jonah. I belong
with them.'

'But you belong with...' Jonah stopped himself.
'I...I'll miss you, Dad. I love you.'

'I love you too, son,' said Jason, 'but it is time we
said goodbye.'

Jonah didn't want to do it. He didn't want to lose
his dad. Not all over again. But he knew that what
Jason had said was right, and what was more – and
maybe this was because he could still feel the other
Uploaded and their shared sense of love in his head
and in his heart – he felt he would be able to accept
it this time.

Jonah and his father embraced. For the longest

time; the final time.

Eventually, Jason stepped back and spread his dragon's wings wide. He looked up to the sky and, like sand flowing through an hourglass, his avatar dissolved into its component pixels. Those pixels hovered in place for a second and began to glow. Then, as Jonah watched, they scattered and joined the dance of the lights around him, until he could no longer see which of the lights had been his father.

Goodbye, the collective voice of the Uploaded whispered in Jonah's head, and this time he thought it sounded like his father's voice. And he thought he could hear his grandmother in there too, and so many others.

Goodbye, Jonah. Goodbye, our saviour.

A ring of light opened, bigger than a halo. It was a portal, a portal back to the vast white room. He felt as if the light was pulling him towards it. Back towards where he belonged.

Jonah turned away from the darkness and the dancing lights. But he stood a moment longer on the threshold of the portal and he held onto the feelings of the Uploaded in his heart, pledging to himself to remember them all.

This is what I need to remember, Jonah told himself, *this feeling right now. Because I know I'm going to miss him, every day of my life, but I'll always be able to come back to this moment and I'll know...I'll know that, in the end, he was happy.*

He took a deep, shuddering breath and flew into the light, knowing that he'd never see his father again.

38

Jonah awoke in the real world and found himself in Sam's arms.

'I…thought you were…gone,' she stuttered.

'We lost you on the monitor as soon as that monster sucked you in,' said Axel.

'I tried to hack in,' said Luke, 'to get you outta there, but that squid wasn't opening up.'

Slowly, Sam released Jonah and he explained what had happened. He hoped he had conveyed just what it felt like it there – but he knew his words were insufficient to describe the experience he had just lived through.

'So we're finally safe from the Uploaded?' said Axel.

Jonah nodded. 'But are the Uploaded safe from us?'

The question hung in the air. Jonah remembered thinking that there wasn't anywhere in the world safe for the Uploaded. Even now that they were contained and content, they were still vulnerable in five grey boxes. They could still be hunted down or erased. There had to be another place, somewhere the Uploaded could live on, in their collective consciousness, free from any hacking. But there was nowhere on Earth...

Then it hit him.

There was nowhere on Earth. But what about above it? High above it.

Jonah rushed back to the deck and leapt off the beached barge. He raced across the sand, where just two days ago he was at war, and searched the line of pirates, calling out for Howie. He spotted him helping a group of pirates carrying micro-servers to a new boat.

'What's the big rush, Jonesy?' called the pirate leader, meeting Jonah on the beach.

'The Uploaded are safe and contained, but they can't stay here.'

'No argument there,' said Howie.

'No,' urged Jonah. 'I mean, they can't stay here... on Earth.'

'What are you...' began Howie, before a big smile crossed his face. 'I get it,' he said. 'You want me to—'

'To be a rocket scientist again,' said Jonah. 'Send the Uploaded to the one place they'll be safe from us.' Jonah pointed to the sky.

'Our satellite,' laughed Howie.

'You were preparing to put it into orbit, to track the ocean. Can you add the micro-server to it?'

'You know, I was going to cancel that launch, now that we're legitimate business people and all.'

It was Jonah's turn to smile; he caught a glimpse of the excitement in Howie's eyes.

'But you really want to launch that rocket,' Jonah speculated. 'Don't you, Uncle Howie?'

'You bet, Jonesy. You bet.'

It was already hot, although not even seven a.m., as Jonah stood outside the control centre at Cape Canaveral Air Force Station. He was waiting for the rocket to launch. Why be this close to something so spectacular, he reasoned, and only see it on a monitor?

Howie and the pirates, along with Sam and Axel, were inside the control centre. That suited Jonah. He wanted to be alone.

It had taken weeks for Howie's crew to ready the launch. In that time, Lucky Luke had left Miami, on a chartered private plane that would take him back to Manhattan.

'My offer's still good,' he had said to Jonah. 'Your adventures'll make one heck of a game.'

Jonah didn't like to think of all of the danger and death he'd experienced as a game. This metawar was so much more than that. But then, he'd remembered how much fun he'd had as a kid, blasting away at Luke's brain-sucking zombies or flying spaceships through asteroid belts, and wondered if maybe a game version of everything his father had lived through would somehow keep Jason alive in the minds of the players. They wouldn't know, of course, that it was all real. To them, it'd be fiction, just a game. But if Jason's red dragon could be programmed into a Lucky Luke game, maybe, in a strange way, he'd achieve another type of immortality.

'OK,' Jonah had agreed. 'Just be sure to tell the whole story.'

'You got it, pardner.'

In the end, Jonah was glad to see Luke leave, however much he liked the cowboy. He reminded Jonah too much of the last person to inhabit that body.

The pirates had been prepping the satellite launch for a year, using the disused NASA facilities and a secret stash of rocket fuel. Howie had explained that when Florida had started to unravel, he and his fellow NASA scientists pledged to save the space facilities from the rioters and looters. When they'd turned to piracy, he'd planned to use the satellite to have his own private surveillance on the world's waterways. Now he was planning to use the same satellite to keep the distributed servers of the Eastern Corner operating, and to house five very precious pieces of cargo: the micro-servers containing the Uploaded in the squid.

Howie's voice boomed through a tinny loudspeaker just above where Jonah stood:

'In 5…4…3…2…1…ignition!'

Right on cue, the rocket's engines burned and

smoke billowed out around it. Jonah found himself holding his breath as the rocket rose into the air. A minute later, it jettisoned its first-stage engines and fired the second with a thunderclap boom.

Jonah's gaze was drawn to the rocket's core fuselage, the cylinder that housed Howie's satellite. The rocket's flight, for all of Howie's planning and preparation, would be a short one. It would soon come crashing back down to earth. But the solar-powered satellite – and the micro-servers lodged inside it – would orbit the Earth forever.

Jonah's father, a lifelong pilot, was taking the ultimate flight.

Howie's voice returned to the loudspeakers and, in solemn tones, recited a poem that Jonah remembered his father sharing with him when Jason was away on long flights:

Oh! I have slipped the surly bonds of Earth
And danced the skies on laughter-silvered wings;
Sunward I've climbed, and joined the tumbling mirth
Of sun-split clouds,— and done a hundred things
You have not dreamed of — wheeled and soared and
     swung
High in the sunlit silence. Hov'ring there,
I've chased the shouting wind along, and flung
My eager craft through footless halls of air. . . .

Up, up the long, delirious, burning blue
I've topped the wind-swept heights with easy grace
Where never lark, or even eagle flew—
And, while with silent, lifting mind I've trod
The high untrespassed sanctity of space,
Put out my hand, and touched the face of God.

Jonah hoped – no, he *felt* – that somehow, in some impossible way, his dad knew that he was slipping the surly bonds of Earth and that he was enjoying the ride.

The rest of the Uploaded too, he thought. *This is for all of them.*

He kept watching the rocket until it was no more than a speck, high up in the sky – and even longer, until it had travelled way beyond the range of human sight and even its smoke trail slowly dissipated on the breeze.

'Goodbye, Dad,' whispered Jonah.

He felt Sam's hand slip into his. She was standing at his side, looking up to the heavens.

'Take care of him up there, Mum,' she said.

Epilogue

Jonah leaned on the bow of the Guardians' barge as it pushed north through the rolling waves of the Atlantic Ocean.

The vessel sailed north along the dark Florida coast. Sam and Axel were in the wheelhouse with Captain Tiller. The barge seemed huge without the stacks of micro-servers on its deck. It seemed empty. Jonah tried not to think about how empty it felt without his dad.

Jonah took in the enormous size of the night sky around him. He was watching the distant stars, hoping to see a moving one. Howie had told him that, at certain times of the year, under certain conditions, it might be possible to glimpse the satellite containing the Uploaded.

Jonah had no idea if this was one of those nights.

He heard footsteps on the deck; they stopped a short way behind him.

'Hello, Sam,' he said, without turning around.

She leaned on the bow beside him. 'I'm sorry. I didn't mean to disturb you.'

'It's OK, you didn't. You aren't.'

'You didn't want to be alone?'

'I'll never be alone,' said Jonah. 'Wherever in the world I go, I'll always know my dad is up there, watching over me.'

'Yeah,' said Sam. 'I feel the same way about my mum.'

They sat down cross-legged on the deck, keeping their eyes fixed on the night sky.

'It's funny,' said Sam. 'When we get to the Northern Corner, it'll be the same sky, looking down on us. The Uploaded will be up there and we'll be down here, fighting.'

'I'm so sorry, Sam.'

'You did what you thought was right; you couldn't haven known that Andrea would—'

'No, not about the usurping, though I am sorry about that.' Deep down, Jonah was still ashamed that he'd failed to protect Sam in Havana. 'I just couldn't kill her, even though she would have killed you.'

'Are you talking about Havana?'

'I wanted to protect you,' he said.

'And you did,' said Sam. 'You never stopped.'

'I wonder if maybe you're better off without me,' said Jonah. 'The Guardians know where the Northern Corner is; you don't need me for that any more. Maybe I should sit this one out. I just mess things up. It's like you said, I'm not a fighter.'

'I never said that, Jonah,' said Sam. 'Andrea did.'

'In your body,' said Jonah. 'She was reading your thoughts.'

'Yeah, she was. But she read them wrong. Look how hard you fought for the Uploaded, Jonah, even after they betrayed you. You fought for us when we were captured by Howie and his pirates. We'd have lost the Eastern Corner if it hadn't been for you. And as for all the times you fought for your dad—'

'But in Havana—' began Jonah.

'You couldn't shoot a woman in the back,' said Sam. 'So what? The one thing Andrea got right is that it wasn't your fault.'

'But I—'

'But nothing. Jonah, you are one of the bravest, most determined and resourceful fighters I have ever known. What you aren't is a cold-blooded killer. There's a big difference.'

'Maybe,' conceded Jonah.

'Definitely,' countered Sam. 'So, OK, maybe the last thing you want to do right now is pick up a gun again. But I want you at my side. I need you at my side, Jonah.'

'Really?' mumbled Jonah.

'It's your choice, of course. If you want to quit while you're ahead, no one would blame you for it. But we've been fighting for a future we believe in and we're not finished yet. So long as Matthew Granger and the Millennials are willing to fight, and kill, for their future, we haven't crossed the freedom frontier.'

Jonah's eyes strayed skyward again. He couldn't help it.

And Sam must have noticed, because she added, 'If Jason were here now, I know he'd tell you to do what you feel you have to do. He loved you, Jonah, and I know he was proud of the man you've become.'

'You really think so?'

'There's no question about it. You could see it in his eyes whenever he talked about you. Of course your dad was proud of you.'

'No, I mean…you…you think I've become a man?'

Sam didn't say anything. She just smiled.

As Jonah gazed up at the stars, eager to see that one spot of light, his father now amongst the heavens, the boat chugged relentlessly north carrying them to what Jonah hoped would be the freedom frontier.

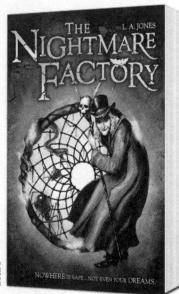
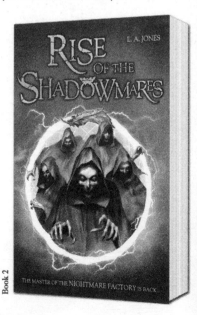